THE
PARACHUTE
DROP

THE PARACHUTE DROP

NORBERT ZONGO

TRANSLATED FROM THE FRENCH

BY

CHRISTOPHER WISE

Africa World Press, Inc.

P.O. Box 1892
Trenton, NJ 08607

P.O. Box 48
Asmara, ERITREA

Africa World Press, Inc.

P.O. Box 1892
Trenton, NJ 08607

P.O. Box 48
Asmara, ERITREA

Book Design: 'Damola Ifaturoti
Cover Artwork: Sean Kilpatrick
Cover Design: Roger Dormann

Library of Congress Cataloging-in-Publication Data

Zongo, Norbert.
  [Parachutage. English]
  The parachute drop / by Norbert Zongo ; translated from the French by Christopher Wise.
       p. cm.
  Includes bibliographical references.
  ISBN 1-59221-202-6 (hardcover) -- ISBN 1-59221-203-4 (pbk.)
  1. Burkina Faso--Politics and government--1987--Fiction. I. Wise, Christopher, 1961. II. Title.

PQ3989.2.Z587P3713 2004
843'.914—dc22
                              2003027989

Translator's Preface to *The Parachute Drop*

by
Christopher Wise

In the Winter of 1997, Norbert Zongo offered a public lecture at the American Cultural Center, adjacent to the U.S. Embassy in Ouagadougou, Burkina Faso. I looked forward to attending the lecture, after following Zongo's weekly columns in his journal *L'Indépendent* for nearly a year. It was always a pleasure to read Zongo, who often published under the pen name Henri Segbo, and whose articles were noted for their brutal honesty and good humor. The University of Ouagadougou was at that time embroiled in a strike, which was a subject of daily debate and gossip among locals. The room that evening was packed, so I was forced to take a seat near the back. Zongo spoke in a quiet voice on the subject of journalistic freedom and responsibility. What struck me then was the calm with which he described the numerous attempts on his life, even joking how he seldom rode in the same automobile twice. The Burkinabè government's favorite method of eliminating its political opponents had been to attack its enemies in their cars, for instance, a car bombing in the case of Professor Umarou Clément Ouedraogo, or machine gun fire in the case of Professor Moktar Tall.

Everyone in the room knew Zongo was not exaggerating, and it was comical, in a horrifying way, to hear the misadventures of the bumbling Burkinabè soldiers who had failed to kill him. Zongo spoke like a man who knew they would, of course, get him in the end. He had carefully considered this question from about every possible angle: he knew what kind of man Blaise Compaoré was: he knew how many people Burkina Faso's president had already killed, and it seemed unlikely that he could escape Compaoré's henchmen forever. Men who had offended Compaoré in far less serious ways had already been killed. This was probably the reason for the calm with which he spoke that night: he spoke as a man who had looked death in the face and was not afraid.

That same week, I went out for drinks at the Wassa Club with a friend who was a diplomat at the French Embassy. We often went to dance clubs together, or dined with wives, girlfriends, and others in Ouagadougou's best restaurants. My friend and I rarely discussed politics, only the student strike had become such a news item that it inevitably came up. I was teaching at the University of Ouagadougou and now found myself with time on my hands. This is why I could stay out late, night after night, following Ouaga's lively night scene. At last I brought up the subject of President Blaise Compaoré. I had just read an atrocious biography of Compaoré written by a French toady named Jean R. Guion, including a preface by the French Ambassador. "This book is absolute shit," I said to my friend. "You people know that Compaoré is a murdering villain, and yet you continue to support him and lie for him."

"I don't know about that," my friend said. "Compaoré is not as bad as some."

"He's killed a hell of a lot of people. Professors, for starters. He killed this student president, Dabo Boukary."

"Well, life is pleasant in Burkina Faso, right now. Don't you think? If one or two people die, it's still better than what you have in Liberia." He was already bored with the topic. I had violated the terms of our friendship. We ordered another round of drinks and changed the subject.

But a year or so later, when Norbert Zongo was killed in a car bombing along with three others, I remembered my friend's nonchalance, his *boredom*: men are often killed in Africa, especially writers. It is an old story, not even worth more than a brief notice in American newspapers. Steven Biko would be forgotten today if Denzel Washington had not played him in a B-movie. Ken Saro-Wiwa already seems forgotten. The fact is that the first world has little interest in such questions. But once the expendability of those who "write what they like" is acknowledged, we cannot so easily dismiss their words. From Zongo's *The Parachute Drop*, General Kodio puts it this way, *"A man who is staring at death can become a veritable oracle."*

The words of Zongo ring with a certain power because they reek of death. He does not ask anyone to pity him; he cares nothing for our pity. He merely has a few things to tell us, things that are known only by the condemned.

What Zongo offers us in *The Parachute Drop* is a complex portrait of an African dictator. It is a book that horrifies, that offers no easy solutions to the contemporary nightmare of African politics. Still, Zongo's novel is not merely cynical, for Zongo was not a cynical man. He believed that concrete solutions to Africa's social problems were possible. In the pages of this novel, he sketches out a few of them for us. They are problems that he tirelessly wrote about in his journalism as well as in his imaginative prose.

First, Zongo suggests that one of Africa's greatest problems might well be the poverty of its political discourse. President Gouama, as well as his real life counterpart President Compaoré, are of course monsters of gargantuan proportions. Nevertheless, the more urgent target of Zongo's novel seems to be the language used to both valorize and villify Africa's leaders. For in the end, Gouama is only a man, albeit a man with demonic energy and malice. The revolting way in which Gouama is first celebrated and then torn down, only to be replaced by another "Beloved Leader and Guide," overwhelm the reader with a nauseating regularity. Zongo will not even deign to narrate the fake political crises of the novel; instead, he lets the obnoxious mouthpieces of Watinbow's media falsify what is already false to begin with, badly staged events waxed over by an even more fraudulent abuse of language.

As Zongo insisted in his political journalism, freedom-of-speech is not enough. Free speech also implies a certain responsibility, a responsibility to accurately report the facts (Zongo's maxim was "the fact is sacred"), but also to recognize the humanity of those one writes about. Open, democratic discourse must be temperate, fair, *humane*. This is why Diallo, one of the students who saves Gouama's life, implores him to desist from bludgeoning students with the label of "Marxists." "If you feel that you've learned something," Diallo tells Gouama, "teach all those who label others 'Marxists' and 'revolutionaries' what harm such words do, how they needlessly divide African peoples and distract them from the real battles that confront us."

Is it possible to disagree and yet acknowledge the humanity of one's interlocutors? This is a question Zongo urges us to ask ourselves. This is also why, even in his most sardonic and bitter moments, Zongo refrained from simply demonizing even a well-known assassin like Blaise Compaoré, the man he knew would surely kill him.

Second, Zongo clings to the belief that the spheres of the public and private, at least in the case of Africa's political leaders, may not be sundered: it is incumbent upon those who run Africa's governments to sacrifice their personal desires in the interests of the people they serve. For Zongo, this means that the political leader must be morally *superior* to the common man; he must even be a kind of "super-ethical" individual, impervious to the overwhelming temptations for personal gain that will inevitably confront him. This is not to say that Zongo advocates the eclipse of the human individual, merely that those who chose a life of public service must relinquish certain personal freedoms. The medical student Mamadou does not reproach Gouama because of his incredible lust for money and women (although he does not of course approve of these things either) but for his abuse of the trust the people of Watinbow have extended to him.

"What example did you set for the people when you were in power?" Mamadou asks Gouama. "If you presume to guide the destiny of others, you must be willing to sacrifice your own destiny, your own personal desires." Zongo himself makes this point in one of his political essays, stating "If a leader hopes to impose his moral vision upon others, he must himself be able to recognize the difference between right and wrong, between mistakes and crimes. Above all, he must not commit such crimes himself" ("Mobutuization" 2).

Finally, Zongo attacks neo-imperialist agents from the outside that harm Africans in direct and indirect ways. The most blatant example in *The Parachute Drop*, also targeted in canonical texts like Frantz Fanon's *The Wretched of the Earth* and Sembene Ousmane's *Xala*, is the problem of the outside "advisor" like Marcel and his boss "the Ambassador." A large portion of the drama turns around who will gain control of Gouama's Swiss bank accounts, foreign assets, and other illegally invested wealth. It is of course well known that African leaders like Mobutu Seko Sese, Felix Houphouët-Boigny, Blaise Compaoré, and others have extorted millions of dollars from their nation's coffers with the help of foreign "advisors" like Marcel; but the familiarity of this problem does not make it any less urgent today.

Although Zongo never identifies the nationality of Marcel and the Ambassador, it is difficult to imagine these men as anything other than French. In the specific case of Burkina Faso, the role of the French in shaping national politics – for instance, the rise and resilience of the Compaoré regime – is a question worth asking. When asked in a recently published interview why Compaoré is able to stay in power, given the fact that he is so widely disliked by the Burkinabè people, a student leader bluntly responded, "The French. If the French stopped supporting him, he wouldn't last very long" (Wise "Chronicle" 32).

What must be emphasized here is that the French have not been held fully accountable for the crimes they have committed, and that they continue to commit, in Burkina Faso. It is not an exaggeration to say that Blaise Compaoré, like Gouama, Dagny, and Kodio in *The Parachute Drop*, is literally the creation of French foreign policy in West Africa.

However, Zongo also points to more indirect forms of neo-imperialism, specifically targeting the IMF and World Bank. If these institutions have been the focus of attention by activists against globalization at recent WTO conferences in Seattle, Prague, and elsewhere, Zongo – like many other African writers – fixed his attention upon them long ago. In *The Parachute Drop*, the men and women who run such institutions are compared to "terrorists" in their detrimental effects upon the African people.

Mamadou complains to Gouama of a "terrorism that comes from London, Paris, and Washington.... [T]he terrorism of those who determine the value of our labor, of those who have never seen a coffee plant and yet fix the price of coffee on the market.... Those who get rich on our misery are the real terrorists... The terrorists who harm us live on Wall Street, in the business districts of Paris and London. Our enemy is the IMF. Our islamic jihad is against the World Bank."

For North American readers, this means we are by no means let off the hook by gesturing towards corrupt French foreign policy. There is a sense in which we ourselves, by our indifference, by strategically averting our eyes from such problems, are implicated in Zongo's killing, for it is these financial agencies – often at one with French advisors like Marcel — that have cleared a path for dictators like Gouama, Compaoré, and countless others.

Zongo's *The Parachute Drop* is a significant contribution to African literature. It offers one of the few sustained meditations on the psychology of the African dictator and therefore encourages its readers to imagine an Africa delivered from such tyrants.

In closing, I would like to acknowledge the important contributions of Richard Priebe, Edris Makward, Ann George, U.S. Ambassador Jimmy Kolker, Virgil Bodeen, Beth Willey, Kathryn Stevenson, Sean Kilpatrick, Judith Wise, Geri Walker, Damola Ifaturoti, the Bureau of Faculty Research of Western Washington University, and the members of the African Literature Association. I would also like to thank those Burkinabè citizens who helped make this translation possible. For obvious reasons, I cannot name them here, but they know what they risked in helping me, and they know why it was worth risking. I would also like to express my disgust for certain individuals who did everything they could to hinder this project. To you Burkinabè citizens, may your miseries and misfortunes multiply with your remaining days!

Works Cited

Fanon, Frantz. *The Wretched of the Earth.* New York: Grove Weidenfeld, 1963.

Guion, Jean R. *Blaise Compaoré: Realism and Integrity.* Paris: Berger-Levrault International, 1991.

Ousmane, Sembene. *Xala.*

Segbo, Henri (pen name for Norbert Zongo). "Mobutuization," L'Indépendent, N. 193 (1997): 2.

Wise, Christopher. "Chronicle of a Student Strike in Africa: The Case of Burkina Faso, 1996-1997," *African Studies Review*, Vol. 41, No. 2 (1998): 19-36.

For Further Reading

Harsch, Ernest. "Burkina Faso in the Winds of Liberalisation," *Review of African Political Economy*, Number 78 (1998): 625-641.

Sankara, Thomas. *Thomas Sankara Speaks.* New York: Pathfinder, 1988.

Stevenson, Kathryn, "The Legacy of Norbert Zongo," in *Sankofa: Perspectives on African Literatures at the Millennium,* Edited by Arthur Drayton. Trenton, New Jersey: Africa World Press, forthcoming.

Tall, El Hadjj Sékou, "Key Concepts and Traditional African Society," (translated by Christopher Wise), *Voices: The Wisconsin Review of African Literatures,* Issue 4 (2000): 55-63.

Wise, Christopher. "The Killing of Norbert Zongo (1949-1998)," *Research in African Literatures,* Vol. 31, No. 1 (Spring 2000): 232-233.

——. "The Killing of Norbert Zongo," in *Sankofa: Perspectives on African Literatures at the Millennium,* Edited by Arthur Drayton. Trenton, New Jersey: Africa World Press, forthcoming.

——. "Writing and Freedom: The Zongo Affair," *ALA Bulletin: A Publication of the African Literature Association,* Vol. 26 (Spring 2000): 83-86.

Zongo, Norbert. "The Mobutuization of Burkina Faso," (translated by Christopher Wise) in *The Desert Shore: Literatures of the Sahel,* Edited by Christopher Wise. Boulder, Colorado: Lynne Rienner Publishers, 2001: 158-173.

Preface by Norbert Zongo

"Who asked you to write about the President?"

Before I could reply, a blow struck me across the face. Another, more violent assault followed. Then another flurry of blows. I covered my face in my hands. It was noon, not morning, not evening. March 27, 1981. It was like the beginning of time for me, the day my life began to melt like butter on a hot skillet.

"Why did you write about the President?"

Despite the buzzing in my ears, I understood his question well enough.

"Who says I wrote anything?" I had the courage to say. "Where's your proof?"

The gendarme, a representative from the special police, angrily jerked open his drawer. He hurled a crumpled envelope at me. I scooped it up and, without even opening it, dared to ask, "Who's it addressed to? Which president? Is it a tract or a letter? It doesn't even have a heading. In fact, it isn't even signed. Why would anyone write the president simply to insult him? What purpose..."

A fist struck me so hard it knocked me out of my chair. These were the last questions I dared to ask before my year in detention began. I spent three months that year in solitary confinement, which began three days after my interview. I was labeled a "serious threat to the State."

"You are a dangerous subversive. Because of you, four hundred students are now threatened with expulsion. Worse still, you are an anti-militarist radical, an extremist fanatic. Your political writings are complete shit. If it's proof you want, look at this..."

The gendarme dropped a large packet on the table. I read _The Parachute Drop_. It was a manuscript I had mailed some five months earlier to Editions CLE in Yaoundé. Although I wondered how _The Parachute Drop_ wound up in the hands of the special police, I had learned by now to hold my tongue.

In fact, it was then that I learned the truth about a certain kind of power in Africa, as well as the suicidal nature of all opposition, of all protest in our land. Most importantly, from that day forward I understood that it was my duty to fight this power, to struggle for a more humane Africa. An Africa rid of detention centers, death cells, and torture chambers. An African rid of Founding Presidents, Clairvoyant Guides, and Single Party States.

For I will never cease to believe that a day will come when African people will be able to march freely through their streets, holding protest-signs aloft. In that day, strikes will be held not merely to protest the reign of cancerous and mediocre regimes, nor to simply react against tyrannies that masquerade as "democracies." Instead, protest will come from those who wield a wholly different kind of power, a power that they themselves create and make legitimate. Only then will underdevelopment vanish from our continent.

CHAPTER ONE

An indifferent sun cast its sleepy eye upon the waking city. The horizon glowed with purple light. Day was born anew in a jarring world of merchants, butchers, priests, bakers, meuzzins, and laborers. The bulky frames of the sparse buildings gradually emerged from the morning mist that engulfed the city.

A new day dawned: another reprieve for millions of the world's afflicted. Another reprieve for millions of Africa's unemployed and wretched. For these, the morning would bring yet more troubles, further miseries to add to their years and days of bitter toil. A reprieve for Africa's teaming masses, as well as her more obscure wretches, those forgotten souls who languish in the filthy holes of our Founding Presidents and Clairvoyant Guides.

Another day began: another day of incredible good luck for thousands of people for whom life has refused nothing, for Africa's wealthy and educated, for those who believe it is perfectly normal to exploit their brothers and sisters, to treat their fellows like beasts of burden. Another day for Africa's moral cripples.

Another day began in a world of intolerable paradox, a world where the gods are summoned forth by demons, where spirit is measured strictly for its cash value. A world of incomprehensible duality in which good and evil go hand-in-hand, where heaven and hell exist in close proximity. A world where starving skeletons jostle alongside the grossly obese.

A world of the eucharist and the bitter pill.

In Africa, the world of the President God and his military. The world of *homo-applaudicus*.

It was in this world that the armies of beggars took their places outside the big banks, hoping for random coins to be tossed their way, desperate for pocket change, so they might live to see another morning.

The buildings themselves seemed to come to life. Already, they had swallowed up countless people, workers as well as the unemployed, men, women, and children in search of their daily bread. The stairways resonated with the shuffle of footsteps. The banging of typewriters, like the sound of machine gun-fire, merged with the shrill ringing of telephones and the human voices of the African workplace.

But not all buildings shared the same ambiance. In the city center, beneath a sloping hillside, stood a single tower in the midst of a vast courtyard. This building was distinguished by its unique architecture and by the rows of armed men who encircled it, cutting it off from public access. Seen from the exterior, it could easily be mistaken for a temple, church, or mosque. The calm that reigned throughout the courtyard was impressive.

It was actually a bank, a treasure chest where the State, the "nation" and the "people," guarded their most inestimable prize: their Illustrious Son, Clairvoyant Guide, Founding Father, Beloved Leader, the man who who had single handedly created it all, the architect of the "nation's" prisons and its lone ruling party.

The creator of everything.

It was a powerful factory of propaganda and executive decrees, the headquarters of the nation's most "dearly beloved son." It was the sanctuary from which the fatherland had sprung: a mighty fortress and castle. It was the temple of the President God Gouama, guardian of the destiny of several

4

million people, a shrine to the Democratic Republic of Watinbow.

But let us dispense with all this chattering: The God is at work...

* * *

A heavy voice crackled over the intercom: "Monsieur Marcel, Marcel, Marcel... Mr. Counselor.. Are you there, Marcel?"

"Mr. President! I'm coming, your Excellency! Right away, your Excellency! At your service, Mr. President!"

Marcel had been on-hand from the day the President of the new Republic of Watinbow had disembarked from a DC6, waving from the top of the gangway to the hysterical crowd of well-wishers. Gouama had stood amid the sound of drums, musical instruments, and rifle-salutes. In his hand, he brandished a shiny leather bag for the eyes of the immense throng, shouting to all, "I bring you independence!"

The celebrations and dances had gone on for several days and nights. In the churches and mosques, it was carefully explained that independence did not mean the coming of Satan, as it would have had the Marxists gotten their way a few years ago. Father Paul, one of Gouama's most trusted advisors, had stood in his black robes and preached in the capital's largest cathedral how God would surely reward the people of Watinbow for refusing these Marxist devils.

Nonetheless, at the crowded airport that day, a few critics could be heard mumbling skeptical remarks about Gouama and the shiny leather bag he held up to celebrate his victory. The bag seemed too small to contain much of value, but maybe there was a chunk of gold inside or some magical talisman? Was it a symbol of independence? President Gouama never revealed what was in the bag that day, but it had to have been something special. One glance at the gendarmes and presidential guard, zealously keeping all onlookers from getting too close, was all it took to see that.

Since the arrival of the president's DC6 that day, Mr. Marcel had served as advisor, faithful friend, and sincere partner to the new president. It was his task to help the president guide the country during the early days of independence.

"Where were you, Marcel? You must inform the Ambassador that I'll be attending the next African Unity Summit in ten days."

"Yes, Mr. President. You're right, your presence at the summit is indispensable. There are grave crises which threaten the very existence of the organization. In fact, your lucidity is desperately needed. It might well be that your attendance will provide the cement that will prevent the edifice from crumbling. If you like, I can begin writing your speech this evening."

"Hold on, Marcel. I think we better talk to the Ambassador first. Are you sure your country won't reverse its position on any of the problems to be debated?"

"I'm absolutely certain, your Excellency. There will be no reversals."

"You're probably right, Marcel. It's always the same old problems, isn't it? You don't think those obnoxious Saharan Marxists will create difficulties for us?" Without waiting for an answer, Gouama sighed deeply. "Ah, Marxism! It's the scourge of our times. These Marxist students with all their propaganda are like disease-carrying rats. Our entire world bleeds from this Marxist ulcer. Wherever you find it, there's no peace and quiet. If you hadn't kept me from all traffic with the Marxists since independence, I would have been up to my neck with this child of Satan," he added. "We'd be swimming in it."

"Like I've always said, your Excellency, you would've created countless enemies for nothing."

"You're right about that. It's always these idiots on the government's payroll that want socialism."

"Mr. President, let's not return to this tired discussion. I sympathize with your disdain for Marxism, but..."

"Of course you're right. It's my seminary training... No, Marcel, it's more than that. All men capable of telling gold from copper, as they say in my language, are capable of understanding that Marxism is the biggest catastrophe in human history. Every time I get near one of these Marxists, I get this odd feeling. I can't quite put it into words."

"You couldn't be more correct, your Excellency. It's like we've always said. Apartheid is a terrible thing, and the Israeli occupation of Palestine must be resolved. But neither South Africa nor Israel have harmed the world anywhere near as much as the Marxist countries."

"I couldn't agree more, Marcel. Unofficially, you know very well that many of us have a good working relationship with the authorities of South Africa and Israel. And then, South Africa and Israel have such good doctors."

"As your Excellency has known from the beginning, the breaking of ties with Israel has been one of Africa's biggest diplomatic blunders. Africa failed to realize that the Arabs will always prefer to pour their oil dollars into the West, to buy more pretty toys, rather than help Africa out of its misery. The shabby subsidies that they dole out from time-to-time can never replace Israeli technical assistance."

"It's a waste of time even speaking with these Arabs. To get even a thousand dollars out of them, outside of building another mosque or Qur'anic school, you have to wake up at the crack of dawn and go to bed after midnight. Whenever you visit them, they proudly lay out their insulting riches, as if to say, 'Hold out your palm and beg if you want help.' They'd like us all to behave like the little Muslim children who go around begging for alms. On top of everything else, these Arabs are racist to the core."

"Mr. President, the Arabs are only interested in enjoying the spoils of their wealth, in living the idyllic life that their oil money has brought them. All they're really interested in is the teachings of their great prophet. An Arab will follow the voice of his prophet when he's sitting atop his camel or donkey, but put him in a Mercedez with tinted-windows, and he becomes a different man altogether."

"Regarding my speech," the President said. "I would like some strong words condemning South African apartheid and calling for peace in Chad. Ah, poor Chad! There's a country completely destroyed by its own foolish sons."

"Is that everything, your Excellency?"

"Put in yourself whatever I missed. Wait, I forgot something. You must add something about a homeland for the Palestinians. These insufferable Palestinians! Time and again, they've been tricked by the Marxists, otherwise their problems would have been solved ages ago. Too bad for them is all I can say! Anyhow, we must briefly mention their case. If we're lucky, Israel will have stopped bombing them before the summit begins."

"Your Excellency, I think it would be wise to say something about the New Order of Information."

"As you wish. Whatever will help our image on the outside..."

"I've prepared an itinerary for your trip, your Excellency."

"Already?"

"Yes, Mr. President. You'll be flying into Paris, Bonn, Bruxelles, London, and Dakar. Then from Dakar, you go back to Paris and then home again."

"Magnificent, Marcel. It's as if you'd read my mind."

"You flatter me, your Excellency. You know very well I must make the trip myself, to prepare the way for you. At Paris and Bonn, you will meet with some businessmen to discuss their possible participation in certain development projects."

"Over dinner?"

"Over dinner, your Excellency."

"Very good, Marcel. It's always good to do business over a

meal. By the way, I have some good news for you. I succeeded in getting the first installment of the World Bank loan
for that agricultural project in the south of the country. You
will be stopping off in Switzerland..."

"Of course, your Excellency."

President Gouama broke out into loud laughter. "I don't
have to spell it out for you, do I, Marcel? You always understand right away. This time, it's ten million dollars. The Bank
would only release seventeen million. I'm giving one million
to you, for your next vacation. Ah, Marcel, I like you very
much. Thanks to you, I'm a happy man... Now, let's have
none of this false modesty. You've done a great deal for me,
for my family, and my country."

"It's a great honor to hear you say so, your Excellency, and
it brings me great happiness. My only wish is to serve you well
for as long as you need me."

"You've forgotten something very important regarding
Paris. Can you guess what?"

"Oh yes, your Excellency, you must forgive me. We've
not resolved the problem of that land in the provinces you
wanted to buy."

"Come closer, Marcel. I want to whisper it in your ear."
They shook with laughter before the President continued, "You
must find me a really fine one this time, my friend. I want one
with big tits and a really nice ass. Price is no object. But no
Sahelian types. No dried-up, black women. If you find one
like you found last time, grab her. She was a really sweet piece
of ass. That one could coil around you like a snake and then
suck you dry. Ah, these white women! They really know a
thing or two. Comparatively speaking, black whores are worth-
less. They just lay there like dead wood...

"You know, this is really starting to be a problem for me.
My marabout forbids me from divorcing my wife and officially
remarrying, no matter how much she bores me. He says she's
my 'star of destiny,' and if I lose her, I will lose the presidency.

You can imagine how I suffer because of this woman. Figure it out for yourself. A woman you married when you were a petty government bureaucrat can't possibly do you any good when you're president! Look around me, all my peers have changed. The women I associate with now could be presidents themselves. Ah, this subject depresses me. Let's speak of something else."

"You can count on me, your Excellency. I'll do everything I can to help."

"One other thing. While I'm in France and elsewhere in Europe, I'd like to review the cases of our dissident students. I want to make sure that not a single one of them succeeds in getting their diplomas."

"I will contact their rectors and professors to see what can be done."

"Contact their landlords too. It would be helpful if they could be expelled from their lodgings right before the exam period. I'll give strict instructions to all my ambassadors."

"I've already arranged matters with the police. You can rest assured in this matter. These reactionaries will end up in jail where they belong."

"Ah, Marcel, my old friend and brother. You never forget anything. Everything is always done to the letter. I really love your thoroughness. I'll certainly say something about that next time I decorate you. We'll have to process some of these political prisoners when I get back from the summit. We must study each and every case to serve the maximum possible punishment. Nothing short of thirty years for that medical student Coulibaly and all the others responsible at the office for the National Movement for Students and Children. Their luck has officially run out. Now that the Ambassador has pulled back, they are off the agenda. Too bad for the Marxists."

"Precisely, your Excellency. I wanted... Well, I mean..."

"What is it, Marcel? Go ahead and speak."

"I'm counting on seeing your Excellency this evening about

a terribly urgent problem that has arisen. But we must be far from eavesdroppers... It's a quite serious matter."

"Really? Close the door behind you and tell me at least a little. You seem preoccupied. What's it all about."

"It's about... It concerns a situation that has developed from the inside..."

"It isn't possible! We've already replaced all the questionable characters in the unions with loyal militants. The party is perfectly healthy. Where could any opposition come from?"

"The problem has side-swiped us, your Excellency. One of our agents, a technical assistant who teaches at a high school, stumbled upon a dangerous student movement that's won the support of many in your army. The reports we've gotten from this agent have been verified by similar ones we've gotten from inside the military."

"You've got to be joking! Marxists in my own backyard!"

"It's a simple case of subversion, Mr. President."

"There is no subversion without Marxism..." The President's face showed his confusion. However, his surprise soon gave way to anger. Two enormous creases appeared across his massive forehead. The veins on his temples swelled. Finally, he grabbed the telephone and hurriedly dialed a number.

"Who are you calling, your Excellency?"

"I'm calling who I must, Marcel. When he comes, you'll know soon enough." Gouama looked like he would burst into tears, but his voice betrayed no emotion. "This is just terrible," he said. "Terrible..." Suddenly, he exploded in anger, addressing his advisor. "Find out everything you can about this movement. I want a complete list with the names of everyone involved. I want all of them hanging from a rope before sundown. Shot! Their throats cut! We will... We will..." The President collapsed in a heap upon his desk.

"Please, your Excellency. You must calm down. We already know everything we need to know. We have nothing to fear from these students, who are mere children. It's the military we must be careful about. The man who heads this group of rebels is not without experience. In fact, he's among the top officers in your army. He may well be the best officer you've got."

President Gouama lifted his head from his desk, his eyes aflame. "Tell me his name!" he shouted. "We will hang him tonight! First, I must phone the Ambassador. How many sympathizers does this dog have? Don't just gape at me like I was wearing a mask! Answer me!"

"Calm down, your Excellency. One must take precautions when dealing with the strong. The guilty one is Commandant Keita, head of the paratroopers."

"Commandant Keiiitaa? Keiiita? Ke-i-i-ita. The man I love and admire more than anyone? My own officer, from the old days, my most faithful and surest officer? Keita wants to dipose me, to kill me, kill *me*?"

"Keita is preparing a diabolical coup. Everyday, he wins more sympathizers to his cause, telling his soldiers that the nation's leaders steal from them and bully them, by keeping up a ridiculously low standard of living. He tells them that the army is an army of nepotists, that the only ones who can hope to rise to the level of sergeant are those whose family members are in high ranks. Then he tells them that the army is now organized along colonial lines and that, under you, they're little more than *tirailleurs*, like in the old days. He disclosed to the soldiers that your Chief Staff Officer diverted all the money for the new military camp that was supposed to have been built. He even confirmed that you..."

A loud knocking on the door interupted Marcel.

"Come in," Gouama cried.

The Chief Staff Officer of the army entered, standing in salute with mummy-like stillness.

"Just a minute," said Gouama. "How long does it take you to get from your office to the Presidential Palace?"

"Five minutes, your Excellency."

"And you think it's been five minutes since I phoned you? Listen, Kodio, do you even know how to read a watch."

"Yes, your Honor. I must apologize. There was a traffic jam."

"Well, you're here now. Tell me what's going on in that army of yours. The army I entrusted to you."

"I have nothing further to add to Mr. Marcel's report, your Excellency."

"You know what's happening then?"

"The treachery of Commandant Keita could not pass unnoticed. But the Ambassador and Mr. Marcel instructed me to say nothing until we had gathered all the evidence. Now we have it."

"And so my army wants to overthrow me, to dispose me, to kill me. What rank had you attained when you quit the colonial army?"

"I was a sergeant, your Excellency. Only a sergeant."

"Precisely. You were only a sergeant. A pack of jobless good-for-nothings that I rehabilitated to form an army. That's all you were. It was me who saved you from misery, from unemployment. And this is all the thanks I get? A *coup d'état?* I gave all of you a second chance to march again, as soldiers. And now this motley crew of unemployed *tirailleurs* wants to take my power from me?"

"Your Excellency. You know that I have always followed you and remained faithful. I will happily swear my allegiance anew." Lieutenant Colonel Kodio fell to his knees and even clasped his hands, as if in prayer. He bowed his head before speaking. "I swear to God, upon my word of honor, that I will always serve you and only you. I swear it upon the grave of my father."

"Get up, old sergeant, get up. I know it's not your fault. It's mine. Why did I have to go and form an army? I should've let you all remain tailors, farmers, and taxi-drivers. Then there wouldn't be problems like this one. What is it that you people want? One of your old army buddies, a man I saved from oblivion, thinks he's now fit to be president. I give him the rank of colonel, but that's not enough for him. Here's a man who's fit to be little more than a dog-catcher and now, three years after independence, he's thinks he's a good candidate for president."

Gouama's anger grew even more intense. "Where were you army people when we were fighting for independence? Where were you when we were fighting Paris, London, and Bruxelles? Where were you when we brought liberty to the African people?"

"Nowhere, your Excellency. We were nothing. It's you who made us what we are. We accomplished nothing without you."

"That's not quite true. Not entirely. For you know very well that your asses were buried in the mud of the Sahara and the sand of Vietnam. Your stinking asses were rotting in filth." His entire body shook with anger. Gouama paced the room and then stood for a moment behind Lieutenant-Colonel Kodio. Suddenly, he kicked Kodio in the seat of the pants. The kick was so vicious that Kodio fell face down on the floor. Gouama then pivoted around and fixed his gaze upon his advisor Marcel. He thought he detected the hint of a smile on Marcel's face. "Why do you laugh, Marcel? Are you making fun of me?"

"Not at all, your Excellency. Certainly not, Mr. President. I'm simply confounded by all of this. And, in your anger, you got a little mixed up and said 'the mud of the Sahara' and 'the sand of Vietnam.' That's what made me smile."

"You are easily amused, Mr. Advisor. Or perhaps you're simply an idiot? Or a madman?" President Gouama returned his attention to Kodio. "Tell me, Sergeant. What were you doing while the rest of us were fighting to liberate this country, to gain independence for our people? Were you fighting somewhere in Algeria? Or was it Vietnam? How many recruits entered the army that year?"

14

"Two-thousand, five hundred, your Excellency. Just as you wished."

"Two-thousand, five hundred new recruits. Or should I say, two-thousand, five hundred candidates for the presidency? The single greatest error we made in Africa was to create armies. Armies to parade." Gouama sweated from every pore in his body. His hands behind his back, he paced back and forth across his office like a caged lion. "Do you even know how to read, Kodio?"

"Yes, your Excellency. I await your command."

"Open up the armoire behind you and take a book off the top shelf. The one entitled, *My Vision of the World*, by Albert Einstein."

"Your Excellency. I see a book entitled *How I See The World*, by Albert Einstein."

"You've read this book?"

"Oh no, your Highness."

"And you really believe you're fit to be President of the Republic?"

"Certainly not, your Excellency..."

"Shut the hell up! Open the book and read the first sentence on page fifteen. Read it in a loud voice."

Kodio read haltingly, "*The worst of all gregarious institutions is undoubtedly the army. I abhor all armies.*"

"Read it again," Gouama barked. "Read it until I order you to shut up."

Kodio repeated the sentence in a firm and loud voice. Gouama continued to pace the floor, absently fidgeting with his papers, pens, paperclips, and other objects. His body trembled all over. "That's enough! Now read the sentence at the bottom of the page."

Kodio cleared his throat and read, "*I despise any man who can take pleasure marching in rank to the sound of music. Such a man doesn't deserve to have a human brain or even a spinal cord... Armies are the curse of civilization.*"

"Read it again!" Gouama barked, his eyes bulging from his head. "Again!"

Kodio read so intently that not even a loud knocking at the door stopped him.

"Who is it?" cried Gouama.

"It's Tiga, your Excellency."

Goauma relaxed at last. The very name 'Tiga' seemed to have a calming effect upon him. "Come in, my dear Tiga. I've been anxiously awaiting you. Come in and hear what I have to say. They're preparing a *coup d'état* against me. I've given my life's blood for this country, for my people, and this is how these good-for-nothings repay me. With a *coup d'état*!"

"You said a *coup d'état*?"

"You know very well what I said."

"What bastard would even dare..."

"Who would you like it to be, Tiga? The Senegalese *tirailleurs*, no doubt. One of them not far from here has already declared himself emperor, the lousy thieves!" Gouama turned again to his Chief-of-Staff. "Kodio, do you know the word that best suits the human species?"

Kodio looked to the sky, as if for inspiration.

"The word is *homo sapiens* though in Africa one cannot really speak of *homo sapiens*," Gouama said, "not without some irony anyway. Here you will find instead the *pouvoirdocus leopardis*. Of course, the *pouvoirdocus* is a dangerous creature no matter where he's encountered, but here in Watinbow, we have ways of dealing with the *pouvoirdocus leopardis*. Do you even know what I'm talking about, Kodio?"

"Please instruct me, your Excellency. I'm a mere illiterate compared to you. I know nothing..."

"Imbecile! You won't find the word in the dictionary. It's the scientific name that I've given to the African military man. Perhaps you're forgetting that I once studied Latin? Now, to return to the *pouvoirdocus leopardis*, Marcel. It seems that the most venerated of my officers, the commandant Keita, a ser-

16

geant who won a name under the banana-trees of Indochina, who was later discharged so he could be a farmer in his village, is after my hide. In those days, his entire fortune consisted of a rusty canteen, two worn-out khaki uniforms, three billy-goats, and a few chickens. It is this sergeant who thinks he's now fit to be president, president of Watinbow! A country I created with my own hands. President! I saved this man's life! Today, he drives a Peugeot 505. And what does he want now? My head! My power! Marcel, exactly how many of these traitors are there?"

"We have the complete list, your Excellency, and it's a long one. Bear in mind that Keita was made second-in-command by Commandant Ouedraogo from the same unit."

"So Kodio and Marcel, how should we treat these scoundrels? Kodio, you go first."

"Your Excellency. We have drawn up a plan of action. But with your permission, I'd like to let Monsieur Marcel speak for both of us."

"You've drawn up a plan of action? Why not do what we've always done? Fire bomb them in their cars over the weekend. If that doesn't do the trick, we'll finish the job once we've get them to the hospital."

"We could try, but it wouldn't be a sure thing with either Keita or Ouedraogo, Mr. President."

"Alright. Why don't we organize a banquet and poison them?"

"You know, your Excellency, these two don't like formal ceremonies. They have a kind of sixth sense about such things."

Tiga, the President's special advisor, at last spoke up. "Why not take them out with rifles then? Or maybe a bazooka? Even a canon if necessary? Why not?" Tiga shook with anger. It was Tiga who coordinated and executed the sacrifices demanded by the team of sorcerers and marabouts who had surrounded Gouama since his rise to power. Tiga's bony face and long, hanging mustaches gave him the appearance of a sick man. His bulging adam's apple seemed to throb from under his enormous eyes, which would fix themselves on each victim, as if he longed to devour all those he saw. Under his vest or his large boubou, he always wore a little cotton shirt that was covered with amulets. On each finger of his left hand, he wore no fewer than two rings. His outlandish garb and strange appearance would have inspired a painter to fill his tableau with a multitude of colors.

Tiga's life was inextricably bound up with that of the President.

"Let them speak, my dear Tiga," said the President. "Go ahead, Marcel."

"Mr. President. We've done everything that can possibly be done. Certainly, we could move to eliminate them as you've suggested, but we prefer that they have absolutely no suspicions. There could be hidden sympathizers, waiting for a chance to strike."

"Alright, enough theories. What should we do?"

"Calm down, your Excellency. We're here to help you. There's absolutely nothing to worry about. We've taken every possible precaution..."

"Calm down, you say? Calm down? Go ahead and let them kill me, you mean. Do you realize what you're saying? My life and throne are in danger and you tell me to calm down. You and the ambassador better pay attention. If your country enjoys a close relationship with mine, it's only because of me. If I take a fall, no one will be able to keep these Marxists in check. They will centralize everything. Your middle class compatriots with a chip on their shoulders will all be expelled from Watinbow. It's that simple. You'll find yourself unemployed, even while the country is being ruined by shoddy technical advisors. Those people can't even manage a wheelbarrow yet they call themselves 'technicians.'"

Marcel at last showed signs of nervousness. "Mr. President, all of this is happening because you refused to listen to me in the beginning. From the very start, I urged you not to expel our army. You refused out of pride. You wanted to be surrounded by your cousins, your nephews, and other relations. You have refused to confront these problems. You wanted an army that could promenade in front of you, that could pay you homage. Well, you got what you wanted. You have nothing to complain about. I am no racist, but I recognize the difference between the races. Excuse me for saying it, but the black man is ungrateful. It's not me alone who says so. Even your own proverbs say the same thing. The black man lacks foresight, good sense. I don't fully agree with Jules Perry who says, 'The black will sell his bed in the morning because he doesn't give a thought to where he'll sleep that night.' But it must be admitted that certain blacks lack consistency. I hate to say it, Mr. President, but you have been careless."

"I see, so on top of all my other troubles, you see fit to insult me now."

"Not at all. But I cannot permit you to blame your own errors on me and others like me. Why don't you rely upon foreign military support even now? You're the only one who can answer that."

"I am independent. I wanted to create my own army. How could I have known these dogs would turn on me?"

"It's not too late to do the right thing, Mr. President. You'll get your country back, once this trouble's passed."

"There's no guarantee I'll even get the military support you describe. The order isn't yours to give. But if I don't get help from you," Gouama warned, "there are plenty of others who will give it. I know very well who to count on. If your country refuses, I'll enlist the help of Israel. And if that's not enough, I'll organize an army of mercenaries."

Marcel frowned. "This army, *your* army, is already an army of mercenaries. The mercenary is a soldier in the service of a man or a group of men. Your soldiers are in your service, or better yet, in the service of your government, like many other soldiers across the continent who are paid a fee to secure the power of a handful of men. You already have mercenaries. They just don't know that that's what they are."

"A price cannot be fixed for my personal safety. As for you, doesn't your country spend a fortune on its military? You speak of the security of the country, but there would be no security for those of us in power without military support. And then, after independence, all these petty ambassador-re-publics that you have created across Africa would simply dis-appear."

"Mr. President," said Marcel. "Let me ask you a simple question. Who spends more for military support, you or us? In the developed world, we spend millions upon millions of dol-lars for military support. But if you consider our enormous budgets, it isn't very much. Do you realize it costs more to equip one new recruit than to buy a pershing missle? Figure it out with any pocket calculator. We have the means to buy military strength. You don't. I'm sorry to have to say these things, Mr. President, but somebody must. There are some crises that are entirely avoidable.

"So, Mr. President, here's how we have decided to resolve the case of Keita and Ouedraogo. In one week, you will make a visit to the north of the country. A big celebration will be organized there in honor of your coming. There will be a demonstration for you, a parachute drop from your paratroop-ers. The two conspirators will certainly participate in the jump since their families live nearby. And when they make their jumps, an accident is going to happen. Do you understand now?"

"You must excuse me, Marcel. I'm beginning to feel bet-ter already. I was a little disoriented over the news. Have you already chosen a pilot?"

"I took care of that myself," intervened Kodio. "Everything has been carefully prepared. I will personally give the order for those two to jump. Even if I didn't make the order, they're both so attached to their men that they'd want to jump anyway."

"You must excuse me, both of you. I was overcome with anger. I got a little carried away."

"Your Excellency, you have no need to excuse yourself. I swear to you once more my complete allegiance and loyalty. But your excellency, I would ask you to consider changing your personal guard, as soon as this operation is carried out."

"Kodio, you know the guard is made up of my personal relatives. They are completely devoted to me."

"I don't doubt it. They will be silenced for only a brief period. There are certain elements I would like to put to the test, to see if they are truly loyal. I want to ferret out all the hidden rifles and ammunition in the country."

"I have total confidence in you. Just keep me informed of what you're doing." Gouama began to calm down. In fact, he seemed completely exhausted. He slouched over his wet bar and poured a cognac for each of his guests. "Cheers, gentlemen. To our success."

"Long life and long reign to our beloved president!" cried Kodio.

Tiga and Marcel drank in silence.

"My friends, what would I do without you? We won't speak any further of this matter."

"Mr. President," said Marcel, "I offer you my highest regards and reaffirm the unqualified support of my country, the Ambassador, and me. You can count on us without reservation. In fact, I have already drafted the funeral speech you will give in the north, after the jumping accident. Even today, the date of your visit will be announced on the radio. Nothing and nobody could ever take your place in this country. The Ambassador and I promise you this from our hearts."

Marcel drank his cognac. "Now, if your Excellency per-

mits, I ask your leave so I might prepare for my trip to Switzerland tomorrow."

"Goodbye, Marcel. I'll see you tomorrow. I will try and
relax tonight. Kodio, you may also take your leave. Come and
see me tomorrow morning. Above all, say nothing to anyone."

* * *

Left alone with his special advisor, President Gouama re-
examined the situation. "We must resolve this problem immediately," he said. "Tiga, you must go to Nigeria today and
bring me our man from Kadouna. I will designate a special
airplane for him. Pay him whatever he asks. He hates to travel,
so you must insist that he comes."

"I will do what is necessary, your Excellency. The marabout
that I brought from Gao also recommended that we make certain sacrifices. He spoke of an impending crisis. I'm beginning to believe in everything he says. Still, the sacrifices he
asks for are not easily made."

Gouama sat up in his seat. "You're joking, Tiga? What
did he say must be sacrificed, the moon or the sun? What
sacrifice can be too steep to preserve my power?"

"He asks, your Excellency, that you cut open the belly of
a black calf and insert the severed breasts and vagina of a
pregnant woman. All of this must be done in the casket of a
man buried in a cemetery. On the third day, we will extract
three teeth from a skull buried just for you. You must swallow
one of the teeth. The other two will be set into a magnificent
cane that you must carry with you at all times. If anyone wants
to steal your power, they will have to return the three teeth to
their proper place, which will be practically impossible."

"Well, Tiga, where is the difficulty? Even God would not
condemn me for sacrificing two or three people to keep the
country from falling to the Marxists. Besides, nothing can be
done against the will of God."

"You are right, my president. I will organize everything as soon as I return from Nigeria."

"No, I want it done tonight. Go see your men. It should be easy enough other than the breasts and vagina part. Maybe we could find a sick woman, someone spreading a dangerous disease? There can't be any sin in cutting out a diseased vagina."

"Very true, your Excellency. Everything will be taken care of tonight. I'll put off my preparations for the trip to Nigeria. In my opinion, your Excellency, after this storm has passed, we must do what is done everywhere else. Confide all our arms and ammunition to outsiders. And purge the army of every subversive element. In my opinion, we must avoid having officers too well-educated in the army. No one with higher than a bachelor's degree."

"Don't worry. I know how to deal with my *pouvoirdocus leopardis* types. The shock treatment is what they understand best, something strong enough to penetrate their thick hides. The case of Africa is quite serious. The peaceful citizen wakes up one fine morning, only to learn what has happened during the night. He himself and his country have been set upon a new road that will supposedly bring about their development. But the misery never ends. One morning, the fanfare begins. The words 'dear compatriots' or 'dear citizens' can be heard from the radio. Some political group or military council proclaims its assumption of power and the cycle begins again. There might be some raw military recruit who in a few years will suddenly become an important person for his country, even for the entire world. In the meantime, liberty remains nothing more than a promise.

"Each time the sun goes down, the people of Africa wonder how they will survive the day to come. For their destiny passes from one hand to another, announced by way of music and fanfare.

"Tiga, it is my solemn duty to preserve my country and my

people. Even if I must sacrifice twenty-thousand women. I will not hesitate for one second. I will never hesitate to do what is right.

"Go then to Nigeria and save yourself, save all of us. But come back as soon as possible with our man from Kadouna. Let everyone know that I won't need any entourage when I go home today. As you say, after this storm passes, I will send you to Europe. I must initiate you more deeply into my affairs. When one is an African president, one must carefully prepare for one's retirement. Yes, Marcel was right. We have been careless. And it's true that blacks are ungrateful. Our people are extremely ungrateful. How can they applaud these petty mess sergeants who dethrone the presidents that brought them independence?"

"No one will take away our president," Tiga said. "No one!"

"Of that, I'm quite sure. But that doesn't prevent me from taking precautions. As the ancestors say, 'Even if the cat never chases after the chickens, he shouldn't be allowed to sleep in the hen house.' Well, I must go home. What a horrible day this has been! Ah, I nearly forgot. Our children who study in Europe, yours and mine, will be returing shortly. They'll come back to Watinbow for three days, during their vacation. They're bringing with them a few friends from school. Two of them are the daughters of foreign delegates, four are the sons of cabinet ministers, and six others are the children of businessmen.

"The kids told me over the phone that they'd like to show their friends a clean town. I gave immediate orders to the mayor, who promised to clean things up around the town."

"Your Excellency, it appears our children and their friends will be here before our trip up north."

"Certainly."

"I would then suggest to your Honor that we invite these young people to accompany us, so they might see a real African festival. We must, however, take certain precautions to get rid of the beggars in Zam'Wôga. Our reputation might suffer otherwise. We must take these same precautions when the European parliamentarians come. We mustn't take any chances since the foreign press might be coming with them."

"You're right, Tiga. I will contact the governor of the north and the mayor of Zam'Wôga to personally give the orders. All right then, that should take care of everything. Goodbye and bon voyage. I will return to my house but without the entourage. One must use discretion when one liquidates such criminals."

CHAPTER TWO

The stars had just disappeared from the sky like frivolous lovers.The faint mist, late messenger of the harmattan that had lingered for six months in the African Savannah, invaded the small town of Zam'Wôga where some forty thousand souls were already awake, a new feature of their daily routine since they'd learned of the visit of the Founding Father, the President of the Republic. The village had to be cleaned up, and water was hard to come by.

The houses and trees that lined the biggest roads had been painted and repainted, but each day was a new battle against the sand blown in on the harmattan wind, as men and women slumbered deep into the night.

The militants of the party loitered about the streets and in front of the houses. The dying April flowers also came back to life, thanks to the rare gift of water at this late date in the season.

But the busiest people of all were the police. They had received strict orders to empty the town of beggars, lepers, the blind, the crazy. Men, women, and children were crammed together on big trucks that had been sent to evacuate them. Their cries and tears intermingled. Those who were unable to mount the back of the trucks — and there were many — were seized by the uniformed police, who divided them into threes, like so many sacks of peanuts.

Some of the poor refused to be separated from their riches:

a bundle of rags, often concealing a crusty piece of bread, hidden from the vultures that plagued the village. For the beggars, the police relied upon the most persuasive of arguments: the billy-club.

The most wretched men and women wept and even prayed for mercy from a God who had already punished them for their unknown sins.

This spectacle was not uncommon. It was not the first time the authorities had worked overtime to increase the misery of the people, so that foreign strangers would see only the mayors, the governors, the president of a people so deprived of even basic necessities that the baobab was their only shelter during the dry season.

It was not simply from fear that the Western press might report the shocking details of the people's misery that Gouama and his cabinet sought their removal; these poor people also truly irritated the government officials who hoped to make a good impression. The humility of the cynic.

Government officials exercised true ingenuity during such visits to hide the poverty of villages like Zam'Wôga, which sweated misery from every pore, a misery that the harmattan blew in with each new windstorm. The wretched were ever present, visible, and permanent, crying out in their agony, crushed under the burden of their shameful poverty. This poverty had to be concealed from the outside world. Books and newspapers could speak of it, demonstrations could even be held, but Gouama and his subordinates must never be reproached with this misery, which could not be laid at their doorstep.

The poor huddled together at each corner of the road in their misery and poverty, disguised old skeletons who sold millet cakes or peanuts. They were disguised as dirty young people with matted hair, vendors of cheap junk imported from China, milling about the streets without hope or purpose. However, it was necessary to get rid of all those in Zam'Wôga who too obviously bore the marks of their wretchedness, who too clearly suffered from famine and unemployment.

Early in the morning, they were easy enough to identify, these poor ones. If some onlookers found this spectacle amusing, the case of an old leper woman Tempoka nonetheless brought tears to the vegetable sellers. Her breasts bathed in tears and mucous, her eyes wide with terror, she cried with outstretched arms, branches from a defoliated baobab tree, begging the police officers for mercy, calling them "my sons, my sons..." The police destroyed the little shelter she had built to keep out the sun. Her house. "She's lived there even before I was born," said one of the market women in tears.

Tempoko no longer needed to beg. Her fellow beggars could be counted on to find her an old blanket, old cloth rags for her dress. As for food? She was provided for by the others, "her sons." That morning she was forced to leave Zam'Wôga to go to a village seventy kilometers through the bush. Along with the others who embarrassed Gouama and his men, she would make this long march along a riverbank, far from Zam'Wôga.

"If you keep to the river, you'll have plenty of water," explained the police inspector who was in charge of the evacuation. "There are also water-lillies and fish for those of you who know how to fish. The high costs of hosting our nation's president and his cabinet are such that the mayor can no longer provide us with the luxury of buying gas to pay for your transportation back to the village. Those of you who decide to return must do so on your own. You know that there is no provision in the town's budget to pay for the transportation of beggars. After all, none of you pay any taxes," the police inspector tranquilly concluded. "Good luck, everyone! We must get back for the arrival of the Supreme Guide this afternoon." He sounded the horn of the Land Rover and waived goodbye with a smile.

* * *

The sun had just completed the last portion of its daily course. The first rays that flooded the sky prevented the groups of dancers and musicians from beginning their performance in tribute to their president, who was settled in the furtive shadows of the town's trees. The water sellers made a fortune. The long and difficult hours of waiting had dried out the throats of everyone.

Within little groups, the young gathered near those who wore a water-jug around their necks. The school children, who had been working on the welcome banners since early in the morning, had now abandoned their stations along the road that would bring them their leader Gouama. Everyone listened to the radio to learn the exact moment of the Founding Father's arrival, the Beloved, and Clairvoyant Guide.

"From Zam'Wôga today," the radio boomed, "the voice of independence sounds all across Watinbow. As we previously announced, we will turn the show over to our mobile unit following the entourage of his Excellency, the Great Architect, National Representative, the Supreme Guide, he who fought so courageously for the independence of our people, the liberator of Zam'Wôga. We could never repeat it enough: if this visit seems improvised in the eyes of the populace, it is in reality a carefully planned test to measure the organizational capacity of the people, the speed with which we can mobilize ourselves as our Leader demands. Our nation's Guide wanted to test us once more, the vigilance of the common folk who must be ready at all times, day or night, to be pressed into service to crush our enemies, both on the inside and outside of our country, even beyond our borders where mercenaries and other crooks work to preserve international imperialism. No one can doubt the loyalty of the people of Zam'Wôga, who have come out in record numbers to show their support of the First Son of our country.

"Hello? Hello? Mobile unit? Let us know if you can hear us. Hello? Mobile unit?"

"Thanks, studio, we can hear you loud and clear. Dear listeners, we're happy to report the arrival of the soldiers of Zam'Wôga who surround their illustrious guest, the Father of the Nation.

"Since the morning, a rising tide of people began swelling at Independence Square. Along with the symphony of drums, flutes, balafones, koras, and the melodious voices of the griots and griottes, the sound of rifle fire can be heard from time to time. The ambiance is like that of the biggest holidays and festivals. The entire village has been transformed by the ceremonial displays, set up to greet the Great Architect. Never in the memory of the country's citizens has there been such a massive mobilization of the people. We can only repeat that to you now that our dearly beloved guide is truly adored by his people. We've just learned that the presidential entourage has at last entered the village. Everyone seems very anxious. The musicians have taken up their drums once again. Professors and school teachers calm their students who are lined along the road. We now hear the sirens of the motorcycle gendarmes who lead the procession. The riflemen along the roadway shoot off their guns, which thunder in everyone's ears.

"He is here! The Great Guide has arrived! The crowd applauds wildly. Seated in his convertible Mercedes Benz, the Father of the Nation responds to all the ovations by brandishing a marvelous cane, and with his ever present smile, the smile of the good chief who loves his people.

"The entourage has just been spotted in front of us. The National Representative descends, decked out in a somber, gray boubou. He salutes the delirious crowd, cane in one hand, and a handkerchief in the other, since it is so terribly hot.

"The Head of State just entered the crowd of admirers. He shakes hands with everyone. This is truly unparalleled. How wonderful to see the president mingle with the common

31

people. Their devotion to him is truly remarkable. The Good Father speaks to his children. He walks among the little school children, offering advice and encouragement. As the ancestors say, 'The most important characteristic of the good chief is nobility of heart.' Our Supreme Guide is a living example of that proverb. What generosity! What goodness! What... What... Well, friends, words fail me at this moment. It's just not possible to describe the love that our Beloved Father is experiencing here today with the inhabitants of Zam'Wôga.

"The walk among the people seems to be ending. The President of the Republic returns to the tribunal, made up of certain members of the government. He mingles now with the high authorities of the region and the town, in the midst of the people's cheers, hurrahs, and fanfare. This crowd is just about delirious.

"The soldiers who organized the celebration tell the drummers and griots to be silent. At last the crowd grows still. The governor of the region, Kouakou Koffi speaks a few words of welcome in an African language to our illustrious host. He recalls the heroic struggle of this man who had the courage to brave countless dangers, to overcome all the obstacles in winning liberty for his people. Our happiness, our prosperity, our development, is due entirely to the efforts of this singularly blessed man, sent by God like a messiah for his people.

"The governor emphasizes one fact above all: the good-heart of our Great Guide, incapable of harming even a single fly. The crowd breaks out in cries of joy. Imagine this, dear listeners, more than a hundred thousand people are crying, applauding, followed by rifle-fire at the end of each sentence. The governor has just finished his speech to the sound of thunderous applause.

"The Supreme Guide, the Founding Father of the nation, the Great Representative has just stood up. The crowd is going wild. The soldiers sing in praise, and now they are joined by the crowd. What fervor! What devotion for our Great

Leader!

"Silence is called for. The Father of the Nation is going to address his people. Listen to our Liberator, our President for Life!"

"Soldiers and supporters of Zam'Wôga, dear compatriots," the President began. "We salute you today in the name of your brother and sister militants at the capitol, in the name of all loyal citizens throughout the Republic. We are very grateful for the honor that you've bestowed upon us today, for braving sunshine, thirst, and wind to greet us this afternoon. Your support is one more proof that, in times of need, the noble ideals of peace, justice, and social progress, the founding principles of our party, are not empty words in Watinbow. Your support today proves again that, in times of need, the goodwill and great maturity of our sole political party are undeniable and irreversible."

Thundering applause broke out again. It continued without interruption, as the crowd now seemed nearly delirious.

"We are here in Zam'Wôga today, just as we have visited certain other villages in the past, and just as we will visit many more villages in the future. It is our duty, in making these visits, in going out among our people, to rekindle the party's flame in the hearts of our people, and to light a way for an even brighter future.

"In the earliest hours of our fight for independence, Zam'Wôga was one of the first villages that responded to the call to fight. The fight for freedom.

"Once again, you have proven yourselves today to be a good example for the rest of the nation. Your legendary passion for hard work, your highly developed sense of honor, dignity, and courage place you in the front ranks of the battle against underdevelopment and its consequences. Zam'Wôga has given the nation strong and valorous soldiers. Perhaps the best examples of this are Commandant Keita and Captain Ouedraogo, whose courage and bravery are legendary."

Applause broke out once again until it was drowned in the clamor of voices and cheers.

"My dear compatriots. It is always worthwhile to be reminded of the strong elements in our party-state, as we are united under the banner that our bravest soldiers carried in the battle against colonial forces, as we fought to win our sovereignty. Ours is and will remain the only party in our great nation.

"For the world that we live in is not only threatened by nuclear war, as well as by more conventional forms of warfare. It suffers not only from economic crises and the misery these crises engender, but it rushes headlong into apocalyptic disaster because of the lack of harmony among peoples. If only the people would realize that their salvation lies in unity, that it is absolutely necessary that all of us work together to attain unity. This is why our party was created. Not only for the salvation of our people, for us here in Watinbow, but to make a modest contribution towards building fraternity and peace among all peoples.

"But as you know, our world often seems like a monkey cage. Whenever one of us strives to build something, someone else will come along and try to destroy it. This is why we denounce all efforts by foreign powers who organize and finance civil wars between otherwise peaceful peoples.

"We affirm here our support for all of our friends who seek peace, not war. But we must be vigilant in the face of the vendors of ideology, the gurus with their theories to undermine our faith in ourselves, in our military. We repeat here that we will show no mercy to those who think that possessing a university diploma or a fancy graduate degree gives them license to cause trouble with the people. The sowers of discord and anarchy, who spread lies and false dreams while claiming they are prophets, these people will be given no sympathy. We will severely punish, with extreme vigilance, all the false prophets of doom with their false beards and false gods.

"Unfortunately, as you all know, our young people today wear their diplomas on their sleeves. The moment you try to give these educated youngsters advice, they turn their backs on you, as if they have all the answers. Here in Zam'Wôga, I make this appeal to all loyal members of our party: You must do everything in your power to unmask and denounce these petty opportunists, who selfishly benefit from the sacrifices of our people and, in return, create disorder and unhappiness. We know that these people are manipulated from the outside by those who are envious of our stability, our peace, and our progress. Order will prevail in our land. We will not fail in this endeavor.

"Dear compatriots, the present international situation and global economic crisis behooves us to make sacrifices if we hope to maintain the high rates of economic growth we have enjoyed in the last few years.

"No one is going to come to our rescue from the outside to build this country for us. We must dream of a better future for our children. This means providing a clear and simple answer to the following question: What kind of country do you want for our children? The future will bring what you want it to bring. This is why, in maintaining our present rate of growth, which is a source of pride and which instills respect among our economic partners, we have decided to retain seventeen percent of high-level salaries, ten percent of middle-range salaries, and five percent of the lowest level salaries. Along the same lines, certain taxes and tariffs will undergo a slight increase. We refuse to heed the call of the IMF, with its cannibalistic remedies, to resolve our problems. We are capable of resolving these problems ourselves, without help from foreign bankers. Loyal soldiers, true patriots, and citizens can only applaud these temporary measures, which will insure the good health of our economy.

"The anarchists and prophets of doom of our nation will no doubt find reason to criticize these measures, as they always seek reasons to agitate and rebel. We have taken them fully into account. We are a state of law and order and we will never tolerate anarchy of any sort. We are committed to the good health of our economy and to the reform of our army, both of which will make us stronger and more productive.

"From this point forward, our soldiers will have everything they need to build an even stronger military. Soldiers of all stripes, the hour for sacrifice and hard work is upon us. It is up to us to save the nation from the whims of international economic powers. We recognize the right to hold strikes for all the workers of Watinbow, but we will put a stop to any strikers who refuse to cooperate with the civil authorities. We are a state of law and order and beware to all those who forget this fact. They will simply have to take their anarchy elsewhere. We don't want it here.

"Dear compatriots. We have every confidence in you. Together, we can overcome every obstacle. Together we will be victorious. We would remind you, however, that the victories of yesterday and today will not necessarily be the same as those of tomorrow. Yesterday's victories are a witness to the past, but they are no guarantee for the future. Our struggles will inevitably continue on into the future.

"Long live Zam'Wôga and its valiant warriors! Long live our party of true leaders! Long live Watinbow!"

The thunderous applause exploded once again, as rifle fire sounded across the sky.

The mobile radio unit resumed its report: "Dear listeners, our Guide has finished his speech. The dancing begins again. What a sight! More than a hundred thousand people have come to praise the Father of our Nation. We've also just learned that there will momentarily be a demonstration from the paratroopers, a parachute drop directed by the valiant Commandant Keita, one of the first sons of this region.

"We now see two airplanes from our armed forces flying at a low altitude. I believe these are the transport planes for our troops. Yes, that's what we're seeing now. The jump should follow soon. The planes are flying slightly higher now. The coordinators of the event are explaining to the crowd what's about to happen. The paratroopers will land on a soccer-field not far from here, a field without fences. Security officers have formed a ring to keep out the curious, who may try to get onto the landing area. The planes are circling now over our heads. All eyes are on the skies above us. The citizens of Zam'Wôga anxiously await the first parachute drop, since all the paratroopers are the students of the Commandants Keita and Ouedraogo, who are the pride and glory of our army. Here they are. It's already begun. One, two, four... Like a cloud of birds, the paratroopers dive into the abyss. They look like little eggs laid by the airplanes. This is quite a sight for those who have never seen a parachute drop before. It's fantastic, a true spectacle. The crowd of onlookers applauds, cries in awe, even skips about. The griots sing praises to the names of Keita and Ouedraogo. The metamorphosis of the little sky mushrooms into men on the ground enchants the crowd. The first paratroopers have landed and now gather their parachutes about them. The second plane begins to drop its cargo of men. What a beautiful sight. Some of the paratroopers seem to be performing leg exercises up in the sky. The announcement has just been made that Commandants Keita and Ouedraogo will also be jumping with their men. The crowd goes beserk with the news.

"The planes begin to gain altitude. They have nearly disappeared now in the clouds. These two veterans of the second world war, of the wars in Vietnam and Algeria, will now give us a demonstration of their talents. These eminent paratroopers who were put to the fire in the jungles of Vietnam and in the Atlas Mountains, are true warriors for our country and for the army.

"A sergeant explains to the crowd that the kings of our paratroopers will be free-falling from the planes, which is why they are flying at a higher altitude now. They will be opening their parachutes only at the last possible minute. From high on the tribunal platform, our Nation's Guide watches the parachute drop. His right hand holds an umbrella to block the sun while he gazes up into the sky. It's clear he's every bit as excited as the crowd gathered today.

"The planes are really soaring at a high altitude now. We can see two small black specks emerging from a white cloud. You really need binoculars, like those held by the Father of our Nation, to get a good look at the acrobatics of our Kings of the Sky. Our brave eagles.

"The two specks become more visible to the eye. They seem more like birds than the two heroes we know them to be. But it looks to me like things are not going exactly as the sergeant had explained to the crowd. Their parachutes seem to be bunched together. I'm not an expert in these things but it looks to me like they're descending at a very rapid speed. The parachutes should be opening shortly... No, no, my God! My God!

"It's incredible, beyond belief! What a catastrophe!

"The parachutes are not opening. There's no doubt about it. It's horrible, it's absolutely horrible! It's incredible! My God! Oh, my God! What a disaster!

"The cries and sobs from the crowd can be heard on all sides. Everyone is in tears. Dear listeners, this is beyond belief what we're seeing here. The parachutes have not opened up and our two commandants have crashed to the ground. It's horrifying!

"Dear listeners, I have been asked to turn over the broadcast to the studio, which will shortly play funeral music for our lost ones here today.

"This is obviously the end of the President's visit. This is no mere accident, it's an absolute catastrophe!

"We will be cutting away to the studio now, which will broadcast funeral music. All regularly scheduled programs have been suspended until further notice by order of the local authorities. I repeat, all regularly scheduled programs have been suspended until further notice by the president of Watinbow.

"Hello, studio, you have the microphone."

CHAPTER THREE

"And so, your Excellency, didn't everything happen as we said it would? Haven't your fears been dispelled? I repeat to you once again that the Ambassador and I will take no chances whatsoever when it comes to your personal security. When your power is threatened, we will not hesitate to act."

"I give to you my hand, Marcel. What would I be without you? Not even a week ago, in this same office, I was nearly undone by a nervous breakdown when you informed me what those bastards were up to."

The door's buzzer interrupted him.

"Come in, my friends, come in! It's my old friends Tiga and Kodio. Please, have a seat, my friends. Let the party begin. Tiga, come sit on my left. Kodio, you sit on my right."

"Your Excellency, I am a mere lieutenant-colonel. I..."

"Since when do you question my orders? I'm the commander-in-chief of the army, am I not? You *were* a lieutenant-colonel. I'm making you a general now. No more discussion! Champagne!"

"Thank you. Thank you very much, your Honor..."

"No more thanks. Let's drink. But, Marcel, there's something I don't quite understand. How will we manage the salary budget cuts?"

"It's all very simple, your Excellency. We need not act until the situation becomes grave. Remind the people that there will be difficulties in the coming days. The situation would be even worse if you gave my country any reason to reduce its foreign aid. For instance, you often speak to the people of independence. Remind them that this means taking responsibility for their own fate. The younger generation of government officials often criticizes us as 'neocolonialists.' Maybe it's time they learn the true meaning of independence."

"You're right, of course. I can't dispute what you say. But you won't abandon us because of a few bad apples, will you? So, let's raise our glasses, friends, and drink to the death of our enemies. May they rot in hell! It was comical, was it not, that we had to cremate the remains of these devils? It was quite funny delivering their funeral orations. It was all I could do to keep from bursting into laughter. On top of that, I order the investigation into their deaths myself!"

The others laughed heartily and even broke into applause. Carried away by the general merriment, Gouama ordered one of the oldest wines in his cellars uncorked for the occasion. "General Kodio, listen to what I have to say. Above all, I want you to be a true mentor for your soldiers."

"You Excellency, your desires are my orders. I swear to you, on my word of honor..."

"I have every confidence in you, Kodio," Gouama cut him short. "What you must understand, what you must drill into the thick skulls of these *pouvoirdocus leopardis* types, is that I am the Father of the Nation. I know they all say it, but they don't really believe it."

"Your Excellency...."

"Shut up and listen. I want you to pound this into their skulls, never let them forget it."

With Marcel and Tiga as his witness, Gouama decided to give Kodio a brief course in political science: "You want to understand what eventually happens to a military regime? Listen. At the beginning, after the initial coup that brings the new regime to power, the early disputes are always about who gets appointed to the limited number of governmental posts that open up. But there is a far more subtle struggle for position that takes place, to see how the 'courageous' men will line up behind the president. These are the 'strong men' in the making, only some are stronger than others. There are the first strongest ones, the second strongest ones, the third strongest ones, and so on. There are always too many 'heroes' after a coup d'état. This is the first phase in the life of a military regime.

"During the second phase, the battle of the 'heroes' goes on behind the scenes: Hero Number Five wants to become Hero Number Two; Hero Number Four wants to become Hero Number One; Hero Number One wants to eliminate all those who dream of taking his place. In this way, the fighting begins anew. The heroes systematically obliterate one other. Each in his turn crashes and burns until a new Strong Man emerges, a shining star, a 'Guide.'

"In the third phase, a single party state is created. You put on a big show for the people, promoting the illusion of democracy. Basically, you do what we're doing right now. The wasp builds a nest, promising honey for all, but the wasp doesn't know how to make honey. All he knows how to do is sting. After the third phase, you end up right back where you started. The cycle starts all over again.

"Now, General Kodio, let me ask you a question. Can Africa really be developed to its full potential under such circumstances?"

"Impossible, your Excellency," said General Kodio.

"The insane spread of military regimes across our continent is the true cause of our underdevelopment. This logic is indisputable. A military regime is always a coup d'état waiting to happen."

"Certainly, your Honor. I see your point."

"What I'd really like, Kodio, is that each and every recruit understands this, that each soldier deeply believes this. Our country has a single party to lead, only one true party that can bring about its highest development. Any other way will lead to disaster. Kodio, you know nothing about politics. Wearing a general's uniform doesn't make a man a politician. I want you to think very carefully about what I'm saying."

"Very true, Your Excellency. Very true indeed."

"At present we have eliminated two traitors, precisely so that other 'heroes' may not get any ideas. Do you have anything to add, Marcel?"

"You're right on target, my President. The other day, when I returned from Switzerland, I went out of my way to see the Minister of Cooperation. The Ambassador will receive instructions from him soon. Everything will be arranged during your next visit. Your power will be protected as need dictates, to make sure you're shielded from the lust for power of all those you wisely call '_pouvoirdocus leopardis_' types. A marvelous and wise neologism."

Gouama blushed with pleasure and then applauded. He was as excited as a child. "Good old Marcel. You never cease to amaze me, old friend. How wonderful! Long live international cooperation!"

"We are at your disposal, your Excellency."

"I know it, Marcel. I know it. Pour me a drink. We must drink to it! Tiga, you must organize a get-together this evening. We must drink, eat, celebrate! Of course, we must not neglect to invite a few of our more destitute young citizens, if you know what I mean..."

Everyone broke into laughter.

"What is your pleasure this evening, your Excellency?"

"We will see. We will see..." Gouama hesitated. He chewed on one finger, his eyes lost in revery as he imagined the young girls from previous evenings. He tried to recall some of their names, but only one or two came to mind. Suddenly, Gouama smiled, "Tiga, you remember the school girl who was with your niece the other day. I saw her at your house."

"I know where to find her, your Excellency, but she only

recently turned thirteen..."

"Nobody asked you how old she was. After all, I'm not seeking recruits for the military. Thirteen years, you say. How many months is that? Tell me, how many months in the life of a thirteen year old?"

"Very well, your Excellency. Consider it done. Now, let's move on to a more urgent concern. It was Machiavelli who said, *'When princes think more of their personal pleasures than the state of their military, they are as good as lost.'* Now that the ax has been laid to the tree, we must make sure no new branches spring up from its roots."

"Speak clearly, Tiga. Less riddles."

"I'd like to say to Mr. Marcel that the elimination of Keita and Ouedraogo is not enough. We must liquidate all those who might follow in their footsteps."

"You're quite right, Mr. Tiga," said Marcel. "I've brought for his Excellency a list of all those who were implicated in this would-be coup. It remains now for us to decide when to strike. Even now as we speak, many of these officers are assembling in the officer's mess hall to talk things over. Mr. Tiga, you must have noticed that those who hatch plots often wear the fear of the gallows upon their faces. Perhaps we should all pay a visit to the military camp tonight?"

Kodio smiled his assent.

"Very well, General. Let us first have another glass of his Excellency's fine wine. While we drink, perhaps we can discuss how to liquidate these children of the great corrupters, Keita and Ouedraogo."

"We should arrest them on the spot," Gouama said, "and then put them in prison with the students we've arrested, since they are as big as idiots as the Marxists. We'll try them sometime next week. Tonight is a night for celebrating. After our party, I'll have the heads of all these Marxists and traitors."

"Your Excellency," said Tiga. "I'd like to suggest we use dynamite and simply blow up the whole lot, while they're meeting. The entire city will hear the explosion. It'll sound plausible if we said it was an accident."

"We'll consider it, Mr. Tiga. But let's first see what you find at the military camp."

The men prepared to take their leave when Gouama, who now felt the effects of the champagne, added, as if by afterthought, "No, I want them all arrested tonight, or tomorrow morning at the latest. Lock them in the cells with the students. There isn't much space for all of them, I admit, but we can take care of that problem easily enough." The eyes of Gouama now sparkled. "The solution is simple. We'll hang the students tonight, every single one of them."

"That would serve nothing, your Excellency," said Tiga. "It would be a pointless gesture. These students may still be useful to us. The other day a sorcerer urged me to make a sacrifice requiring the liver of a man. Since it was late, I sent for one of the students."

"You're right, Tiga. If we have goat farms, why not keep a 'man farm'? Especially if the men in question are Marxists? Very well. Do as you please. Ah, and don't forget to stock my own room tonight, Tiga. I have my heart set on that one I mentioned earlier..."

"I will certainly see to it, your Excellency. But now that I think about it, what of the young wife of the petty official you had me send for after your trip to the north? She arrived at my house last night. You had originally wanted me to bring this one..."

"Out of the question. She must wait her turn until tomorrow night. Anyway, I already promoted her husband to a higher government post in the city. This way, I can keep this little fairy near-at-hand. She's far too fine a specimen for a mere petty official. Her husband will be assigned to the Ministry of the Interior next week, as a technical advisor to the Minister."

"Very good, your Excellency. If you'll permit it, we must now attend to the problem of the traitors. Goodbye, Mr. President. Goodbye, Mr. Marcel."

* * *

The powerful Mercedez Benz of Tiga drove in record time the several kilometers drive to the military installation. General Kodio was the first to exit the vehicle. "Mr. Tiga, don't disturb yourself. I'll first have a quick look in the dining room to make sure they're there."

"Very well, General. As you wish."

The general made a few quick strides until he stood in the middle of a large room filled with men. The officers arose at once from their chairs to salute him.

"Sit down, men. There's no time to lose. Those who I point to now have been targeted for execution. No time for explanations. We will shortly have a guest among us, a guest I've come with and will be leaving with. All those who have a guilty look on their face, who pretend to ignore him, will be slated for execution."

With these words, the general stalked out of the room.

"They're meeting, as we thought, Mr. Tiga. And quite a few of them have guilty looks on their face. They're crying over the deaths of their heroes."

"Let's go," said Tiga. "I must see them for myself."

In the mess hall, Tiga promenaded around, his Adam's apple throbbing, and his owl eyes fixed on the faces of the various men assembled. Upon certain faces, his eyes rested for a long, uncomfortable moment. General Kodio addressed the room of officers, "We have with us tonight my old friend and brother Tiga," he said. "The well-loved brother of our illustrious Guide, the Founding Father of the Nation."

Some of the military men applauded.

"He has come to offer you his condolences over the deaths of our commandants. His time being very limited, he can only stay with us for a few minutes."

Tiga gave a short speech before bidding the men farewell. "I'll be seeing you again very soon," he said with a menacing smile. "Not all of you together, only a select few of you."

General Kodio accompanied Tiga outside. "What do you think?" he said.

"You were right. I saw plenty of officers with guilty looks on their faces. We must act quickly. They must be arrested before tomorrow morning. The non-commissioned officers will be executed the same day. No time to lose. I sympathize with the concerns of Mr. Marcel, who wants everything to happen under wraps. Today, however, time is working against us. You will phone me after the arrests have been carried out?"

"No problem, Mr. Tiga. There will be no difficulties, I'm certain."

"Good. I'll say goodbye then, General. Let us show our gratitude tonight to the man who has made us what we are. Let us liquidate his enemies."

"Goodbye, Mr. Tiga. Consider it done. I'll return to my house where I'll supervise the arrests."

The Mercedez Benz of Tiga sped away once more. General Kodio waited until it disappeared before returning to the officer's meeting room.

"We were waiting for you, Colonel," said one of the officers. "The Ambassador phoned and left the following message: 'There are three eggs in the nest.' He repeated this three times. Mr. Marcel, the President's Advisor, also sent two heavy cases for you with this message, 'Something to hold you till the Christmas season.'"

"Very good. President Gouama gave me a list of suspects to arrest. Here it is. I made a photocopy. The coup is scheduled for tomorrow morning at three. That's why we got the message about the three eggs in the nest. Marcel has provided us with the necessary artillery to proceed. There's no point in delaying any longer. Keita and Ouedraogo, the two who might have opposed us, have been eliminated. With those two alive, we would have had their regiments on our backs. Those dogs were completely devoted to their master Gouama. They would have squelched the coup from the start."

"To speak frankly, if Keita and Ouedraogo were still alive, I wouldn't have anything to do with this coup," said Captain Maïga. "The day you sent me to feel out Commandant Keita, I was terrified. I just about pissed in my pants. As soon as I alluded to a possible coup, the tone of his voice immediately changed. He began making threats against anyone who would even consider such a plan, denouncing such 'anarchists.' 'We are soldiers,' he said. 'Our sole duty is to defend our country's borders. Beware to any petty schemers who even dare to think of such a thing.'"

"I'm afraid he said worse things than that, Captain Maïga. Much worse than that. Here are the plans of the city with the different strategic points we must occupy after the coup. We'll give no quarter to the heads of the militia. We have succeeded in silencing only about half of the president's guards. Our men will liquidate the other half. We're well organized enough to have reinforcements in place for every possible misstep.

"We're also quite lucky tonight, since President Gouama will sleep in the luxury bedroom next to his office. He'll be there with a little girl of about thirteen. He's pretty drunk, so my guess is he won't have even touched the little girl."

"I don't understand why the Ambassador wants him still alive. What does he have planned for him?"

"That's quite simple, Captain Onana. You know that all old African dictators end up in Europe, where the governments welcome them. But have no fear. We are prepared to follow the Ambassador's orders to the letter, with only one exception. Gouama must die. I myself will personally spit upon his grave. I don't want that man alive. There will be no ghosts to escape from our country's political cemetery.

"We will liberate all the political prisoners except the students. We will also restore the salaries of the officials who have lost their jobs. Measures have already been taken to that effect. For now, I present to you the list of the cabinet members of my government. You will find three sets of names: those men who have been selected by the Ambassador. These are the men who are steady and competent. All of them did their studies in European and American universities. They all regularly refused to get involved in pro-Marxist student movements. They are all sound economists.

"It was Mr. Marcel who helped draft the names for this government. All the members of the advisory committee were present.

"Moreover, nobody will be forgotten. After the coup, you will all take a place in the new government. Each of you will be richly rewarded."

"One thing worries me," said Corporal Karfo. "How are we going to get by on such paltry salaries?"

The room began buzzing at once, as each officer similarly voiced this perspective.

"Your question is pertinent, Corporal. Clearly, we will have to revise the present salary schedule. Don't forget, it is quite possible to remain a corporal but with the salary of a commandant."

The officers burst into applause, as a mood of celebration swept across the room.

"I promise you that no one will be shortchanged. But we must make a fresh beginning. We mustn't act as if we will be out of power within a week. It takes time to lay a solid foundation. One must go slowly. For instance, we will not touch the president's automobile park. We'll continue to go about in jeeps. Try and maintain the same rhythm of life. No excesses. We will also denounce the cooperation treaties that bind our country to that of the Ambassador."

"Are you joking?"

"Just keep your mouths shut and listen. It's the Ambassador himself who drafted the declaration that I'm going to read. We will adopt the language of the left."

"What does this mean, 'the language of the left'?"

"It means that we must continue to speak as if we were revolutionaries, Marxists even."

"Like revolutionaries and Marxists? I don't like the sound of this. I'm not in agreement with this at all."

"Calm down, Corporal. It's only necessary that we look like Marxists. You know that the majority of young people today, either from ignorance or stupidity, are attracted to leftist ideas. We're merely being cautious, as a way of drawing in the largest number of supporters. We will pay lip-service to liberation movements throughout the world. We'll name responsible union leaders to a few important posts. But all the while we'll be restructuring the entire army. The old president foolishly remarked that '*A military regime is a coup d'état waiting to happen.*' Nonetheless, we will take some preventative measures. I repeat to you once more: Let's make sure we get the people behind us from the start. Everything else that happens depends on this. Who was it who once said, 'One must organize in such a way that, by the time the people stop believing in your words, they'll have to believe in your might'?"

Kodio thought for a moment. He tapped on his forehead with his knuckles, trying to remember who had coined that famous saying. He appealed to the rest of the officers for help.

"It doesn't really matter who said it," Sergeant Sido said at last. "Whoever said it, we all know it's good advice."

"Very well. Shall we retire now and get some rest? I'll see each of you back here at 23:00 hours. Everyone should come back on foot. We don't want to reveal any signs of our presence. By the way, are we each going to sacrifice a sheep before beginning? My sorcerer tells me the success of our operation depends upon it.

"Let me also repeat, I want that old bastard Tiga taken

alive. We must get from him the names and addresses of all Gouama's sorcerers, so they can be neutralized or possibly pressed into our service.

"Does anyone have anything else he'd like to add? Okay, let's separate then. Everyone should know his task by now. In any event, the most difficult part is behind us. With Keita and Ouedraogo out of the picture, we're free to proceed. Those two were like faithful dogs for Gouama."

One of the officers smiled, "We have nothing to complain of," he said. "Keita even left a pretty young widow for us. I'm already nearly worn out from two little orphans I take care of each evening."

"Be careful there, Sergeant Amouzou. Widows can be deadly. All right, are we ready to hit it? Tomorrow, we will be the most powerful personalities in our country. Good night, men, and good luck."

CHAPTER FOUR

The president's children and their European friends had been invited to a party at the Ambassador's mansion. At the Presidential Palace, in the luxurious bedroom next to Gouama's office, the little girl Hélène lay asleep next to the drunken president. They were both draped under the mosquito netting, bathed in a faint blue light. Hélène, whom Gouama had not even bothered to undress before violating, slept deeply in the luxurious bed, knocked out from the wine she had been forced to drink.

Around eleven 'clock, Gouama was shaken from his slumber by Tiga, who kept doubles to all the president's keys. After Gouama failed to respond to his questions, Tiga dragged the president into the shower. At last, Gouama awoke, yawning stupidly. Tiga forced him to drink black coffee. "No time for explanations," he said. "The hour is grave. One of my sorcerers in the West just came to my house. He's very worried. He has foreseen a grave danger hanging over us. This is why he traveled more than 400 kilometers to warn us. He recommended that I make certain sacrifices, which I did without delay. But there is one more sacrifice that you must perform. You must wrestle against a black donkey, and you must defeat it, before the break of dawn. Otherwise, the coming of the sun will mean the end of our regime."

"What? But Keita and Ouedraogo are dead," interrupted Gouama, who was slowly recovering his senses. "Do you mean to tell me they are alive?"

"Not at all, your Excellency. But I have confidence in no one. Above all, I distrust the Ambassador and Marcel. It's quite common for them to change presidents when they sense a shift in popular sentiment. It seems their country even has a special minister for arranging coup d'états overseas."

Gouama gradually shook off his drunkeness, put on a sports jacket, and stood for a few moments contemplating the body of Hélène, who lay sleeping on the bed. He seemed to hesitate before resolving to follow Tiga. She'll be here when I get back, he assured himself.

Tiga drove the Land Rover, in the back of which lay a black donkey, tied up with cords. Gouama followed Tiga in his Mercedez Benz 600. They drove twenty kilometers outside the city before Tiga stopped. He knew of a glade nearby. This clearing would serve as the arena for the unusual wrestling match to take place.

The sorcerer Sanou had already spent more than an hour invoking his fetishes. When he was finished, he tied an amulet to the tail of the donkey and invited Gouama to begin the wrestling match. As instructed, the president took off all his clothes before approaching the donkey. He asked Sanou and Tiga from which angle he should begin his attack, but the two sorcerers watched without saying a word, not even daring to respond to his questions. He must engage in this combat all by himself, Sanou had decided.

Gouama grabbed the donkey by the tail, clasping hold of it for dear-life, struggling to bring the animal to the ground, as the donkey jerked in a backwards motion. Gouama at last let go of the tail and fell heavily on his rear-end. The blood rose to his face. Pain shot up his back from the base of his spine. He bit his lip and angrily hurled himself upon the animal. For nearly ten minutes, the president was intertwined with the donkey, grasping at its front hoofs and then back hoofs, its haunches, its head and neck. He fought with rage but was unable to subdue the animal. The jackass remained master of the situation.

The president's fat belly hindered him enormously. He sweated and panted like a track-runner. He gasped for breath, resting for ten to fifteen minutes at a time before resuming the battle. Nonetheless, the jackass remained invincible.

The hour of dawn approached. An immediate solution had to be found. Also, the donkey had now become extremely irritated and kicked dangerously about. Gouama suggested that someone help him tie up the donkey's hoofs, but Sanou refused. His rejection was categorical: the donkey must wear nothing except the amulet that had been tied to its tail.

The president then proposed that he be allowed to put his clothes back on, as he was not terribly comfortable fighting in the nude. Out of the question, retorted the sorcerer. It was absolutely necessary that Gouama fight in the nude. He was not even permitted to wear underwear.

At last, Tiga found a solution: they must inject the donkey with a tranquilizer. Tiga immediately sent his "boy," the young man who assisted him, off to the city in search of a tranquilizer.

The group waited for the tranquilizer, and then for the drug to take effect. The wrestling match had not yet started again, when the silence of the evening was shattered by the sound of machine-gun fire. They stopped to listen. There could be no doubt about it. Gun-fire and other explosions could now be heard from the city. The battle had begun.

"It's a coup d'état," sobbed Gouama. "They're trying to depose me. They're after my power. My God, I'll no longer be president. It's not true! It isn't possible! I *am* the president. I *am*..."

He clasped hold of Tiga and burst into tears. Tiga sobbed too for a moment before getting hold of himself. Gouama, however, fell to the ground, where he pounded the earth with his fists. Tiga's boy at last helped him to his feet.

"I'm dead. I'm dead. I'm dead. God help me. Sanou, do something. Invoke the fetishes."

"I'm sorry, there's nothing I can do now. The only thing we can do is save our own skins. You are a man. And a man should confront his destiny with courage and dignity when difficulties overwhelm him. You have even had a bit of luck tonight. If the coup-makers had found you at the palace, they would not have spared you. And, who knows, maybe the soldiers who remain loyal to you will triumph?"

"No, Sanou, more than half my guard was laid-off. And if my guess is correct, their replacements are all coup-makers."

"Then there is nothing more to lose. You must save your own skin. If the Ambassador and Marcel really want to help you, they will send paratroopers and air-support to take care of these sons of the devil, to help restore your throne. After all, you are the Father of the Nation. You will surely stay in power."

"They'll do it, you're right. They have every confidence in me. They'll surely do it."

Tiga still said nothing, as Gouama at last stopped blubbering. Gouama seemed to regain his courage, thanks to Sanou.

"We must drive towards the West, towards my village," proposed Sanou.

Tiga finally broke his silence. "I agree with Sanou. You go west with the president. You can cross over to the Republic of Zakro where President Dagny is a loyal friend of the Father of the Nation. As for me, I'll head south. I will win over the Republic of Watinoma, where his Excellency numbers many friends, who are wealthy businessmen. After that, I'll begin recruiting mercenaries for the counterstrike.

"I'll take the Mercedez of his Excellency, and you two will travel in the Land Rover with my boy. I only have a hundred and eighty miles of bad roads. After that, the roads are all paved. Everyone will believe you've gone to the south."

"We will travel only part way by car," Sanou said. "The

rest of the trip will have to be by bicycle and on foot. It seems pretty clear we'll have to go through a great deal of bush and forest. All right then, let us shove off, Mr. Tiga. No time to lose. From Watinoma, you can try to communicate with us through intermediaries. Maybe you can join us later. I will guard our president like the apple of my eye. Do you have any money?"

"No, Sanou, neither of us has a penny. There are only two pairs of gloves, four amulets, and three tubes of aphrodisiac cream in the glove-box. We're completely broke, it seems."

Gouama went through a crate in the back of the car. He found a bottle of whiskey.

"I put it there myself," said Tiga. "Yesterday, I had to go out looking everywhere for a black donkey. It was merely to quench my thirst."

"You did well, Tiga," Gouama said, opening the bottle. He drank down a gulp and then wiped his mouth with the back of his hand. With the whiskey bottle tucked under one armpit, the Founding Father had begun to feel like a president once again. With a serious voice, he begin to give orders to the others. The two cars drove off at the same moment. Gouama and Sanou took their places in the Land Rover, with Tiga's boy behind the wheel.

"We should reach the river Dina in less than two hours. Go quickly, but try not to ruin the car. We have more than two hundred kilometers of hard travel, before we get to the river."

The Land Rover rolled over the brush and thickets like a steady work-horse. Sanou insisted that they drive in a wide circle to avoid two villages in particular. The car was often caught between trees and low branches, which caused the driver to curse under his breath. He drove in wide berths to avoid the various obstacles.

Whenever the car reached a stretch of land without many obstacles, Gouama took advantage of the opportunity to take a few gulps of whiskey. He began to doze, but the constant bumps from the rocky ride made it impossible to sleep. He asked questions in a loud voice but ended up muttering to himself. Sanou, who was completely occupied directing the chauffeur, had stopped listening to him.

A couple of surprised lions roared and showed their fangs, ready to bounce upon the vehicle, which sped by them. A few meters further, Sanou ordered the driver to stop. He had spotted the remains of an antelope that the lions had been busy devouring. "Honk the horn," he told the driver. It was not worth the trouble, since the lions were already far away. Still, the driver refused to get out of the car to help Sanou carry back the carcass. Instead, he drove the Land Rover closer, so Sanou could easily haul in the remains of the antelope.

Gouama took advantage of this brief stop to doze off. The sun now burned away the storm that had seemed to be gathering on the horizon. The turtle-doves sang of the sun's victory. Far away, the howling of a dog sounded, helping to orient Sanou to their whereabouts. "We are not far from the river," Sanou said. "But before we get there, there is a settlement of farmers who plant in this area during the dry season."

The Land Rover drove in a half-circle before resuming the trek across the Savanah. Gouama, who was stretched out in the back seat, rolled over into the carcass of the antelope but continued to sleep, despite the jolts of the Land Rover. He had now consumed more than half the bottle of whiskey.

One hour later, the Land Rover found itself blocked by the giant trees near the river. There was no doubt about it. They were in the forest now.

The driver stopped the car, cut the motor, laid his head against the steering wheel and fell asleep. Sanou climbed out of the car and made his way towards the river. He washed his face and walked along the water's edge. A crocodile wanting to catch the sun's early rays, splashed into the water at Sanou's approach. The sorcerer realized that he had nothing with him to defend himself, not even a small knife. If this reptile only knew, he laughed to himself.

He walked for more than an hour before finding what he sought: a clearing where there were fewer trees surrounding the river. He broke off a long tree branch and put it into the water to test its depths. Returning to the Land Rover, he had a difficult time waking up the driver, who was completely exhausted from their trip. The driver went to wash himself in the river. At last, the group drove the long detour to find the clearing between the trees.

They were forced to carry Gouama by his legs and arms to get him out of the car. The blood of the antelope had spoiled his sports jacket. He continued to snore loudly, as they set him on the ground.

The remains of the antelope now on the ground beside Gouama, Sanou and the driver gently rolled the Land Rover into the river. It entered with a great splash, as if it would swim across, before it slowly began to fill with water. Big bubbles arose to the surface of the water before the roof of the Land Rover was completely submerged.

The driver went through his pockets, pulling out a packet of cigarettes. He pulled one out and shook his head sadly: only two cigarettes remained. But when Sanou saw the driver's matches, he nearly danced about in joy. "Well done, my brother," Sanou said. "Well done. I was just wondering how we'd get a fire going out here. Well done, indeed. Tell me, what is your name?"

"Jean-Marie. But there aren't many cigarettes left. I'm down to two."

"The matches are all that matters. Now we can cook the meat, and once night comes, the fire will keep away the wild beasts."

The driver smoked one of his cigarettes and went back to sleep. Only Sanou stayed awake. The harshness of his life as a peasant had equipped him with strong powers of resistance.

He was nonetheless more than fifty years old.

After gathering a large quantity of dead wood, he grilled the antelope over the fire and began to look for natural herbs for seasoning. He cleared out a space and, with the leaves from a banana tree, made three beds for their comfort.

Gouama awoke in the middle of the day. With a confused face, his eyelids swollen, he at last noticed Sanou and Jean-Marie, stretched out on the banana leaves. Suddenly, he began to moan. "Tiga? Where is Tiga? Where is he? What are we doing here?"

Sanou held him by the elbow and said calmly, "Hello, Mr. President. This is no nightmare you're having. Last night there was an attempted coup d'état, you remember? At the moment we're fleeing towards the west. Surely you remember now..."

Gouama slowly pulled himself together. His pants, which he'd hurriedly put back on, were filthy from the mud, the pockets hanging out like little drapes. He was barefooted and had completely forgotten his underwear. His clothes were also covered in blood. He believed now that he was indeed living through a horrible nightmare. "This cannot be," he said. "I am the President of the Republic. I am the Father of the Nation. I am the Founder of the Party. This country is mine, mine, mine..."

Like an old stage actor, Gouama wandered about the grass, his eyes haggard, his mouth agape, his arms flaying wildly about. Suddenly, he burst into tears, crushed by the reality of his plight. He sat down on the ground and moaned in pain, "I'm a dead man. They all want to kill me. I'm no longer president. I'm as good as dead."

"Courage, your Excellency. Nothing is lost. We are going to the Republic of Zakro where your old friend Dagny will help you return to power. Tiga will also accomplish great things for you. He's recruiting mercenaries, as we speak. So you see, nothing is lost. Not yet."

Gouama continued to sob. Snot and tears flowed onto his

shirt. He buried his face in his hands and gave himself up to weeping.

CHAPTER FIVE

The coup-makers charged with liquidating the holdouts from the militia were the first to successfully finish their task. They now came to reinforce those who were attacking the presidential palace. Five minutes later, they eliminated the last pockets of resistance among the presidential guard, who had seen their forces cut in half. This was a mere test of loyalty for certain soldiers, according to Kodio. Their replacements, who actually carried rifles without firing pins and with fake bullets, had offered no resistance when their remaining comrades at the presidential palace were exterminated. When the three commandos charged with killing the president forced their way into his room, now glowing with a faint blue light, they emptied their machine guns into the huge bed, draped with mosquito netting. More than a hundred bullets riddled the body of the little Hélène from where she lay. On the city streets, where the fighting now reached its climax, the people were gripped by a collective hysteria. Even the dogs barked crazily, as if infected by rabies. The fighting, which had gone on since six in the morning, had alarmed the entire population. The first persons who had ventured outside returned to their houses at once. During combat, the soldiers and tanks flooded the streets. The people sat riveted by their radios, listening for the news. But the national radio station remained silent. The international radio stations seemed to speak of everything, except the fighting going on in the capital.

After eight hours of fighting, the national radio station began to broadcast a program with military music. In between the music, citizens were urged to remain calm. "Stay in your houses. We repeat: stay inside and off the streets. We will broadcast all the news to you as soon as we have it ourselves." One hour later, the national anthem could be heard on the radio.

"Dear listeners," a voice said, "we present to you the Chief of State, the commander of the armies of Watinbow."

A grave voice began to speak: "My dear compatriots. My fellow citizens. A new day has dawned for our country and its glorious people. A triumphant day of liberty, real independence, and true democracy. For many years, our beautiful and rich country has suffered under the yoke of tyranny. Our leaders have exhibited the grossest forms of egotism, crushing the people and their needs. These false leaders have retarded the development of our country. They have pillaged the nation's coffers, the public's well-being, all for their own selfish pleasures.

"From an international perspective, our country has yet to take its rightful place among the nations of the world, and our hardworking people are considered everywhere like a people who can't take care of themselves, who need to be held by the hand."

"We men of the army, the people's army, who fight for the interests of the people, have assumed power today so we might return to the people what is rightfully theirs.

"For the moment, our former leaders are all under arrest. The tyrant Gouama, however, has fled and is being sought throughout the country. We ask all those with information that might lead to the arrest of this criminal to come forward, to contact the gendarmes or the police. Gouama must be made to pay for his crimes, his assassinations, arbitrary detentions, and tortures. Goauma will pay, for the people demand that he pay.

"All the property of the old regime has been confiscated. The National Assembly has been dissolved. A military committee for liberation will take upon itself the running of the state, until the situation stabilizes and free, open elections can be organized. A large committee will be created to investigate the crimes of the leaders of the old regime.

"Long live Watinbow! Long live the people!"

The national anthem began to play once more on the radio. "Dear listeners, you can now leave your houses to show your support for the courageous men who have delivered our country from the grip of tyranny.

"Come out and show your support for the liberator of the people! Come out in large numbers to show your support for your army. God has sent us a deliverer, a messiah, an incomparable redeemer. Death to the traitors! Death to the corrupt! Death to the tyrant Gouama and his followers!

"When a leader does not listen to the words of the people, they end up making him listen! Beware to all those who muzzle their people!"

* * *

The city was covered with posters. The roads thronged with people who could not contain their joy and their hatred. Mobs of demonstrators tore down all remnants of the former regime, the signs and slogans from the reign of Gouama, under the amused eyes of Kodio's soldiers. As evening approached, a group of students, aided by a random assortment of extremists, tore down the large bronze statue of the president. It took less than an hour to tear it down.

Certain stores were pillaged. The human tide flooded the main arteries of the city, burning posters of Gouama, which were plastered against the electric poles and telephone poles.

A large effigy of the president, suspended from the roof

of his former mansion, sent the crowd into a near delirium.

"Death to Gouama!" they cried. "Death to Gouama!" A young student took off his shoes and began to scale the three floors of the mansion. The mob was instantly electrified by the exploits of the young boy who, with the help of repair scaffolding, climbed higher towards the roof. When he finally made it to the top, the crowd exploded. The climber tore off the effigy of Gouama, which he tossed to the ground.

Three husky men gathered up this final image of the president. They tore out its eyes and even began to eat it, starting with the head. The crowd went beserk. In no time at all, the effigy had been eaten in its entirety.

The mob howled, its hysteria mounting. "Death to the tyrant! Death to the tyrant! Long live the army! Long live liberty!"

The mob: Watinbow's "people" who had sworn loyalty to Gouama, who had relinquished 99% of its voice, who had barely five months ago wished to burn at the stake one of his would-be assassins.

The mob: Watinbow's "people" who perpetually organized demonstrations in support of Gouama and his "avant-garde" party — like the rope supports the hanged man — now demolished the walls of his mansion.

The mob: Watinbow's "people," who assembled for the first time without wearing party uniforms, now proclaimed the coming of a new savior.

Certain members of the militia whom the coup-makers had not yet killed were lynched as scapegoats of the party. Legal proceedings in support of capital punishment for the highest officials of the ousted party were read with enthusiasm by a journalist whose voice was now hoarse from so much shouting.

Military curfew was decreed from six at night until six in the morning, a measure which temporarily swept the mob off the streets. The next day, however, the demonstrations continued as if without break. In the offices, factories, and work-shops, endless discussions were held debating the current situation. The new president Kodio was at the center of all conversations. His courage, his loyalty, his patriotism, his simplicity, and so on were heralded on all sides. At last a man had been found who could lift Watinbow from its economic morass, stated certain wise commentators. In two more years, Watinbow will see entire new blocks of skyscrapers in our city streets, others affirmed.

CHAPTER SIX

The sun came out early, announced by the cooing of the turtledoves. A flock of gray sparrows soared overhead. It was Gouama's third night along the shores of the river, his third night of living like a piece of straw blown about in the wind. He had lived through yet another night of pure agony. Despite the assurances of Sanou, he wasn't at all convinced that those who sought him had no inkling of his whereabouts. Every noise terrified him. In the middle of the night, when an owl hooted from a tree, he awoke his sorcerer-guide in a panic, believing their hiding place had been discovered.

Leaning upon one elbow, Gouama now poked at the glowing embers of the fire. Sparks from the fire leaped up from the wood, reminding him of the fireworks from the first independence celebration that he'd organized. He quickly drove the memory from his mind. What he wanted now was to save his own skin, to hide out for a time in Zakro, until he could regain his power.

For three days, they waited for a boat to come which might take them down the river to Zakro's borders. Jean-Marie suggested they might build a raft, but they had no means of cutting down the trees. In any event, they knew that they must act quickly. The antelope had been nearly devoured, and so the question of food began to worry them. Sanou decided to look for help in the camps of the nomad-farmers who lived nearby. In the first camp, which he found after a day's journey, he was well-received. Pretending to be a peddler who had been robbed along the road, he managed to secure a machete, a sack of millet cous-cous, a calabash, and a blanket. However, there was an awkward moment before he was able to take leave of his benefactors.

"You're from the West, you say? Could you help someone who's trying to get into the Republic of Zakro? We have three young people, our children, who would like to travel to Zakro but have no papers to help them across the border. Perhaps you could find a way? We're prepared to pay you handsomely if you can help us," said the camp elder.

Sanou agreed to help. He could think of no good reason to refuse them. The three young people, all with shaved heads, were as thin as skeletons. They seemed exhausted, but were now ecstatic over their good fortune. They were more than willing to follow this providential guide.

A forth young man, this one more beefy than the others, joined the group before their departure. He claimed to know the river lands up to the border of Watinbow. To catch a pirogue into Zakro, it was necessary to walk for more than a week through the forest, he explained. He agreed to come along to insure that Sanou and his three younger cousins all safely arrived at the border.

The group made their way back along the banks of the river, arriving safely at the site where, according to Sanou, the two other peddlers and companions in misfortune had been robbed by bandits. To their great surprise, there was no one to be found near the fire-pit. Sanou called for Jean-Marie and Gouama at the top of his lungs, but there was no response. The two men were no where to be found. The group decided anyway to spend the night in the same place.

Armed with a machete, Sanou hacked his way through the bushes that surrounded them. He feared that wild beasts may have attacked his companions. He had not gone more than a hundred meters before he heard a growling that startled him.

He held his hand to his ear, his other hand clutching the machete. All his senses were awakened. Slowly, he moved forward, his heart beating like a drum. The growling became louder. What kind of animal was it, he wondered? He dreaded to find out. He felt a cold sensation along the length of his spine. He realized that he lacked the courage to confront the growling animal, if it was indeed a wild beast.

By instinct, he sprinted back to the campsite, crying for help. The beefy young man sprang like a panther, an enormous lance in his hand, a dagger between his teeth. "A wild beast!" cried Sanou. "A wild beast! He's there! In the bush!"

The young man slowly approached. The growling became louder and louder. He aimed his lance for attack. If the beast sprang at him, he'd only have one chance to kill it. But the beast, who was hidden in the underbrush, contented himself with growling. The young man moved a step closer, then another and another step. He came to a standstill, tightening his grip upon the heavy lance. Suddenly, he let out a terrifying scream. All the muscles in his body grew taunt. He repeated his battle cry a second and third time before calming down.

The animal continued to growl. The young man set down his lance and asked for a machete. Sanou realized that he had dropped his machete sometime during his retreat.

The beefy young man slowly made his way into the thickets, believing now that the growling animal must be wounded. He hesitated for a few moments. He could not be sure but he thought he saw something darker than a mere shadow. He raised his lance again for attack. If the animal was an aardvark or was wounded, it was forbidden to kill it with a machete. He aimed his lance, gazing wide-eyed at the dark spot. It would be essential to strike the animal in a vital spot, since some wounded animals get a surge of energy, even after their deaths. The last fang-bite, or the final jab of an animal's horns, were always the deadliest of all for the careless hunter.

Sanou had regained his courage, inching ever closer to the

animal's hiding place. Suddenly, he was gripped with doubt. "Don't kill it!" he shouted. "Stop!" He moved closer still, his heart beating wildly. When he stood a few feet from the shadowy spot, his mouth dropped in amazement. "I think it's a man," he said. "A man..."

The beefy youth lowered his machete. Sanou called the names of Gouama and Jean-Marie. The growling became louder, only they realized now that what they heard was not growling: What they heard were groans of pain and then pleas for help. There was no doubt about it: it was a man. Sanou rushed forward and saw Gouama sprawled upon the ground, barely recognizable.

To all the questions put to him, Gouama responded with groans. His nose and lips, like the rest of his face, was swollen and disfigured. The young men lifted Gouama in his arms and carried him to the fire-pit, which Sanou kindled by poking at the wood.

"Where is Jean-Marie?" asked Sanou.

Between groans, Gouama mechanically gestured towards the river. After examining Gouama's face, one of the young men said, "Those are bee-stings." The beefy one went through his knapsack and pulled out a small packet of black powder. Sanou treated Gouama's wounds with a mixture of powders and herbs provided for him by the youth.

Gouama promptly vomited. He threw up the little that remained in his belly. Not long afterwards, he passed out. Sanou prepared millet porridge to which he added a little meat. "What's your name?" he asked the beefy young man who had served as their guide.

"My name is Diallo. All of us share a common uncle, whose name is Mamadou."

"When we get to the borders of Zakro I will pay you in full for your services. Do you think my friend can travel in his condition?"

"Certainly. After he sleeps, he will wake up a new man.

He'll be hungry, of course, but that's all. He's as good as healed. When he awakens, he'll tell us what happened. But, it'll take many days before his face returns to normal."

"That's not a problem, provided he lives. Tell me, why are you and your friends going to Zakro?"

"We have relatives there, uncles of ours. My cousins are going to Zakro to find work. All of them must save money to pay a bridal-price in the next couple of years. They want to get married. The only problem is they lack the right documents to get in. The best thing to do in such cases is avoid the police altogether."

"Are your cousins sick? They all seem so skinny. I wonder if they have the strength to make the trip?"

"They're a little sick, it's true, but I've brought very good medicines with me. Being skinny won't matter. They'll make the trip easily enough."

When it was time to sleep, Sanou offered to take the first watch. He would awaken Diallo once certain constellations reached the middle of the sky.

Gouama woke up just before Sanou had finished his shift. Sanou raised his finger to his mouth to silence Gouama, who seemed poised to burst into tears. The others slept profoundly. The warmth given off by the fire, along with the peaceful sound of the flowing water, was conducive to deep slumber.

Gouama drank his porridge with a ravenous appetite. Diallo was right; the potion was very effective. Sanou quietly explained the situation to Gouama. "Above all, you must hide your identity," he said. "It's a matter of life and death."

The next morning, the group left with the rising of the sun. For the first time, Gouama seemed to remain calm. In a weak but steady voice, he explained to the group what had happened. Jean-Marie and he had first heard a faint noise coming towards them. Panicking, he ran to hide himself in the bushes. It seemed safest hiding in the bushes, but Jean-Marie chose to stay next to the fire-pit. He seemed not to be too worried. All at once, a herd of buffalo was upon them. Jean-Marie was gored in his rib-cage, his entrails spilling out. He was then thrown into the river, the water instantly turning red before swallowing him up.

Gouama had managed to scramble to the top of the nearest tree. He never saw the swarm of bees that hung like an enormous fruit above his head. After the first shocking stings, he madly climbed back down the tree. But a fraction of a second later, he realized the danger he faced upon the ground. In the end, he chose the torture of bee-stings to being trampled and gored by the buffalo. However, his howling at last riled up the buffalo. Their tails pointing towards the sky, they grew increasingly infuriated. Then Gouama fell from the tree like a ripe apple. He dragged himself towards the bushes to escape the buffalo. After that, he remembered nothing further until Sanou and Diallo had found him.

His pants were torn from climbing the tree. And, since he wore no underwear, his private parts were completely exposed. Diallo dug through his enormous bag, from which he retrieved a needle and thread. But Gouama refused to take off his pants, which would have left him totally nude. At last, Gouama rolled over on the ground while Sanou sewed his pants from behind.

* * *

The first day of walking was long and painful. Gouama was utterly fatigued, despite their long breaks for eating. He had no choice but to continue walking. Diallo insisted upon it. He acted as if he knew every crook in the river and had already chosen the places they would sleep each night.

For over a week, they walked from sunrise to sundown, stopping only to eat their portion of fish and couscous. Before they slept at night, Diallo tossed a dozen fishing lines into the river, which he strengthened with net-traps. In the morning, they fortified themselves for their journey with a healthy provision of meat and fish.

Gouama had never experienced more pain in his life, even from the bee-stings. From the long walk, his feet swelled with enormous blisters. On the fifth day, they had to cross a swamp where rotten leaves were scattered across the sodden earth. Everywhere they looked, they saw huge leeches, clinging to the slimy vegetation.

Each time that Gouama looked at his feet, he found numerous leeches wedged between his toes and along the edges of his feet. Every hundred yards or so, the group was forced to stop to pry these voracious beasts from his flesh. The blood now flowed profusely from his feet. From the start, he had wept as if he would empty his eyes of their tears. Then, with the encouragement of the others, he determined to confront the situation with calm and resignation.

The young men all helped him. They surrounded him, attending to his every need. As afternoon approached, Diallo made a stretcher for him, and Gouama was carried by the others through the swamp.

The young men restored his spirits with their joviality, despite the hardships they all endured on the long march. They told him stories to distract him in clear and grammatically correct French. Sanou also told stories, always with happy endings, where the heroes' sufferings ended joyfully. After living through numerous catastrophes, his heroes were always triumphant; they were men who had lived to tell their tales in happier days.

But Gouama was just about at the breaking point. For three days, he suffered from diarrhea, which Diallo and Sanou seemed unable to cure. "It is due to such a meager diet," explained Sanou to the others. "My friend is not accustomed to eating in such a haphazard fashion."

After three days of diarrhea, the state of Gouama's health became worrisome. It was necessary to search the forest for an herb that Sanou believed would cure him. Sanou was right.

After they found the right herb, Gouama was healed the same day.

The group arrived at a village of fishermen, just as the day's shadows faded, the red veil of the horizon now widening with the sun's disappearance. Between the huts scampered little children and toddlers. The sound of hammers and women's laughter could be heard throughout the village, as the day drew to a close. The fishermen returned from their daily toil, singing in unison with the rhythm of the oars slapping the water. Each time that a pirogue pulled into shore, the children cried out in joy and ran to inspect the day's catch.

Diallo led the group to the house of his friend, who was the chief fisherman of the village. They were all very well received. The chief enlisted the help of his closest friends to serve the group heaping plates of fish and couscous, far more than anyone could possibly eat. "It's an old village custom," said a cousin of Diallo's. "No guest must go hungry."

Gouama at last smiled again. The marsh lands now behind them, he felt that the biggest obstacles had been overcome. Soon they would be in the West, which Sanou knew very well: The West, the border of Zakro, the return of freedom and power. He sighed to think he would soon be in Zakro. Maybe not all was lost, he wondered.

Sanou tested the chief on the subject of the recent coup d'état. "It seems our country has a new president," he ventured. "At least I heard a rumor to that effect while we were on the road. Have you heard of any such thing?"

"I've heard nothing about a new president," the chief said. "I'm not even sure who the old president was. Here, we only know the overseer Landaogo, who comes to tax us. There's also a secretary from the state party who once came to sell party membership cards and collect subscriptions. About ten years before independence, I once traveled to the capital, but it was a very long walk even in those days. I don't walk so far anymore. Everything seemed fine in the capital. There were many cars, I remember. I used to have a radio in those days, but I had to sell it to buy school books and notepads for one of my sons, the only one in the village who left to go to school. The school is about a two-day journey from here.

"So, you see, old and new chiefs from the capital are all the same to us. They take our money one way or another, either through taxes or selling us party membership cards. Our own problems with the government have been resolved. As for these new problems with chiefs, they mean nothing to us. Our biggest problem is the lack of fish. The water in the river has been low and so there have been very few fish. Most of the ones that we catch now are not much good. In the meantime, the markets everywhere are inundated with fish, dried or fresh, coming from who-knows-where. What's worse, the farmers are all so poor now, they can't afford to buy even a single smoked carp. It is very hard for us.

"This year, some of us decided to try farming ourselves. We have done what our ancestors never dreamed of doing: till the earth. Tell me," he said to Sanou, "who is this new chief you speak of?"

"You mean the new president?"

"I thought only white people were presidents?" he said. "Among us, we have only chiefs, not presidents. Isn't that so, Diallo?"

"No, we also have a president of Watinbow. It is a different thing then a chief. This new one comes from the army."

"What happened to the old one?" asked an elder advisor for the chief. The old man was one of the village's most important fetish priests.

"Maybe he was killed?" said the chief. "You know, these white men who govern us are capable of great evil. They are so greedy, so weak, and so corrupt that their own masters who send them here don't even want them to come back home."

"You should have said they are little more than thieves! There has been no real independence in this country, no party to speak for the people," said the old fetish priest. "If you are sick, you don't pay a healer money so he can take care of himself alone. I will not speak of the schools where the children are taken by force. I didn't have to go myself, only because the white priest who built the school, at the time, was believed to be a madman. He told people there was only one god. Our parents thought he was a lunatic because he carried his snot around in a rag in his pocket. What was worse, he relieved himself in a hole that was inside a wooden box. I have heard that this is the fashion now in our cities, but at the time, it was looked upon very badly. You must admit it is strange to carry snot and mucous on a rag inside your pocket."

With his mouth agape, Gouama listened to the conversation between the chief and his oldest advisor. He longed to confess that *he* was the president, not these military thugs who had usurped his rightful place. However, he kept his mouth shut. Glancing over at Sanou, he saw from his guide's expression that he must remain silent.

The chief and his advisor spoke for a long time of the hard life led by the villagers. When Gouama felt overcome with a sudden headache and asked for aspirin, the chief burst into laughter. "What would you do with this pill? In all the village, you won't find a single one. We once saw these pills when a white woman came to live here. She wanted to teach our women how to raise our children. She gave out such pills to our women and children. She wanted to teach us about the nutritional qualities in meat, fish, and eggs. A real nut-case.

"Back when I had my radio, I used to hear such nonsense all the time. To urge a man who is starving and poor to eat lots of meat, fish, and eggs is the worst sort of insult. Still, they are right to mock us for being so poor. After all, before they went home, the whites gave us all their power and money and yet we end up with nothing."

Gouama was having a hard time remaining silent. "The whites did not leave behind all that much money," he said timidly.

"What do you know of this matter, my son? It hasn't even been ten years since the whites went home. And when they left, what did we have then? Where did the wealth go? How many of us could claim to possess a hundred-thousand francs? Not more than ten people in the entire country. But today, men whose fortunes were once measured in roosters and cattle have amassed millions since the white man's departure. These men now live in mansions that you see everywhere in the cities. They are driven about in luxurious cars.

"My son, you are a peddler who travels about and so you know more of these things than we do. Tell us why it is so difficult to earn money? If the whites did not leave their money with the people who live in the cities, the ones they chose to rule over us, we must find out what they did with it. That way, we can divide it among ourselves to relieve our misery.

"Not only that, my son, Diallo says that this new president is a military man. Maybe he was only a soldier when the whites were here. How did he go from holding a shovel to being a president, I wonder? You men of the cities of course know these things far better than us. For us, what's most important is that it rains and that the rain brings us fish."

Sanou rudely pinched Gouama's arm. However, it was unnecessary to keep him quiet since Gouama's headache now occupied all his attention. Instead of aspirin, he was brought a warm beverage to calm the pain between his temples.

"Very well, my son, you'll see that this medicine works wonders. City people often claim that we villagers who live in the bush rely upon the science of sorcerers. Those who say such things are mere egotists. The world has never seen such egotists, I think. They keep us in misery while we're here on earth, and then they condemn us to hellfire after our deaths. Fortunately, they themselves are not God."

Gouama was deeply disturbed by all that he had heard. He looked around at the modest village. He saw a large sprawling of straw huts and children everywhere. It seemed odd that there was not a single aspirin to be found. It must be the fault of the regional doctor and the Minister of Health, he thought.

Despite the hot beverage, his headache continued to plague him. Gouama felt as if someone had whacked him between the ears with a hammer.

The chief at last called for the village healer. After an examination, he concluded that the leeches had poisoned Gouama's blood. The cure he recommended was an injection with the toxic sap of an aquatic herb. With this, Gouama's blood would be purged; however, the treatment would take about a week.

Sanou insisted that they find a faster cure. But the healer was adamant: the treatment would take a week, not a day less.

Diallo and his cousins decided they would wait for Sanou and his sick companion at a village about a hundred kilometers away, in a village where the cousin of an aunt of a niece of Diallo's mother had been married years ago. Above all, they did not want to ruin the chief and his subjects who were bound, according to tradition, to completely empty their larders to feed their guests. The rules of hospitality were unequivocal in this regard.

The second day, Gouama already felt better. He was no longer dizzy and the throbbing in his skull was greatly diminished. That morning, at a very early hour, he helped the men prepare their boats and gear for a day of fishing. Their pirogues, cut from a great tree with rough-hewn axes, glided like silent crocodiles upon the water, little-by-little their long fishing poles and nets gathering in the day's catch.

Gouama admired this spectacle, which broke the monotony of the early morning. The magnificent picture of the river, flattened like a dirty, brown ribbon and speckled by the boatsman, who pulled on their oars and sang quietly to greet the day, filled him with the desire to live again. He had not expected to be so charmed by such a scene, a charm which was not to be found in the huge paintings that hung in his presidential mansion. He had not expected to find such happiness among a people whose pockets were as empty as their bellies, whose bodies were mere skeletons, whose future seemed so bleak. He remembered a quote from an author whose name he'd forgotten: *"I am rich with nothing at all. Having nothing at all is the greatest possible wealth."*

But reality at last triumphed, shaking Gouama from his reverie. He was a deposed president. Like a hunted animal, he was sick, crippled, and vulnerable. The tears began to well in his eyes. He returned to his hut, where he collapsed upon his mat and burst into tears.

The next day, Sanou provided the healer with enough herbs to prepare huge quantities of the potion, which he discretely left upon the healer's door. The first day, the healer refused to even look at Sanou's herbs. The treatment did not merely consist of administering the potion, he insisted. The main thing was the white's of the patient's eyes and his urine. The color of both would determine the exact composition of the potion.

Gouama had grown taciturn. He ate and slept very little. Nevertheless, the state of his health visibly improved. During the fifth day of his confinement, towards the middle of the afternoon, he was awoken from his nap by a commotion in the village. The fishermen who had laid out their nets some thirty kilometers from the village unexpectedly returned at this early hour. Speaking all at once, they told a strange tale about police who were searching for something in the area. Gouama set up with a start, straining his ears to hear. His heart beat wildly, as it had now ever since that first horrible night when he had wrestled with the donkey.

He moved closer to the door of the hut. Squatting low, he laid one ear against the straw matting that served as a door. He could not make out exactly what the fishermen said. The beating of his own heart distracted him.

There can be no doubt about it, he thought. The police were upon him. For a moment, he contemplated running away and hiding, but he had no supplies to sustain him, outside of the mat on the floor. He sat back down upon the ground, put his head in his hands, and burst into tears. He was resigned to his fate.

He waited for the police to burst upon him at any moment. He felt sure that they would come. They were too close at hand. Any second, they would pull back the straw matting over the doorway and seize him. He heard the sound of boots outside his hut. No, it was merely the beating of his heart. Or was it? He couldn't be sure. They must be boots! "But what's taking them so long?" he said outloud. "Why don't they just get it over with?"

The footsteps approached his hut. They resonated over the sand like the hoofs of elephants. They were close upon him now, almost at his doorstep. Seconds passed until he heard a knocking at his door. Gouama put his hand on his heart, gasping for breath. Then he blacked out.

When Sanou opened the door, he found Gouama face down on the ground, completely unconscious. Sanou called for the healer and the chief, who helped to revive Gouama. "You must find a sorcerer to help your friend forget the robbery," the healer said. "He's a complete wreck."

With wide eyes and haggard face, Gouama slowly returned to consciousness, surprised to find himself still inside the hut. He looked around at all the faces but saw no police.

"Where are the police?" he asked in a flat voice.

"They haven't come here," said the chief. "My men say that they will go to a big village about a day's journey from here. By the look of them, they would have searched the village from top to bottom. They came in a big motorized pirogue that stopped all the pirogues on the river and searched them.

"My men did not see them, but the fishermen up river

warned us to avoid them. These men of the law would have confiscated all our fish for their larders.

"It seems they were asking if anyone had seen the old president. As if would recognize him!" The old man stopped and thought for a moment. "It is true one of my wives once saw a photograph of the old president, but how could she remember him from a mere picture? These police promised a boatload of money to all those who helped capture him and death to those who hid him. But none of this is our concern. We are happy to be far from these things. Once again, I see how right I was to stay away from the big village. The administration there serves its own interests, no one else's."

The healer doubled the dosage of medicine for Gouama, who grew stronger with each passing day. His beard hairs also began to grow, like herbs in a valley at the first winter rains. In the nights, Sanou forced him to eat his soup of smoked fish and corn mush. It was essential that Gouama be fully restored to health for the journey in two days.

After careful reflection, Sanou confided to the village chief that he and his companion were wanted by the customs officers and police because of their business, which the administration had deemed illegal. If the police should come to the village, it would therefore be necessary for them to hide from sight. The next morning, at an early hour, the chief decided to hide his guests now, rather than wait for the arrival of any police. He hid each one inside a corn bin.

"If the police come," he said, "you will hear someone hoot like an owl. Cover yourselves entirely with corn, and they will not find you. Don't worry. You are our guests, and you are also friends of Diallo. We will take care of you."

CHAPTER SEVEN

Gouama was cramped inside the corn bin, a little hut built upon stacked piles of wood. The ears of corn were very hard against his buttocks. He considered asking for a cushion but decided against it. Instead, he stretched out his legs and leaned one shoulder against the wall of the bin. He would wait. Tomorrow, they would depart, and after that they would be free. At least, that's what he hoped. There was plenty of air inside the bin, but it was dreadfully hot. Gouama, who was exhausted from his most recent adventures, dozed off and then fell into a deep slumber.

Towards the middle of the day, he awoke again. Footsteps. Many footsteps. He could hear them not far from his corn bin. The steps came and went. A commotion could be heard in the distance.

Gouama cringed inside the bin, his hands trembling. The straw from the corn bin created holes that he tried to see through. It was useless. He couldn't figure out what was happening outside. Feverishly, he wedged his fingers into a hole in the straw walls and tried to widen the gaps. The straw split easily enough, but he could still only see what was directly in front of him. There was nothing except a few hens and a couple of children sleeping on the sand.

The footsteps returned, many of them. Gouama thought he heard a woman trilling. Like a crazed mole, he burrowed down under the corn. The footsteps stopped before his corn bin. Gouama held his breath. His heart beat wildly inside his chest.

"There he is!" cried a voice. "There!" A violent blow from a stick shook the corn bin.

Gouama jumped up, howling and desperately waving his arms for balance. The wood underneath the bin shifted with a crack, knocking it to the ground with Gouama and the corn spilling out. Gouama struggled to free himself from the corn, pulling himself up to escape, but his feet became entangled in his pants, which fell about his ankles and sent him sprawling on his face. The fishermen were absent, all on the river in search of their daily quota of fish. Only the women remained in the village, smoking the fish or pounding corn into cornmeal. They came running at the sound of the crashing bin and the howling of Gouama. But they averted their eyes at the sight of a naked man, who moaned and sobbed in the dirt. Sanou now came out from his hiding place and searched through the ears of corn for Gouama's pants. At last, he succeeded in calming Gouama down. He washed the dirt from the skin of Gouama, since flies had begun to follow him around.

The children explained that they had been chasing a big grasshopper, which had hopped onto the side of the corn bin. One of children had struck at the grasshopper with a big stick to kill it. "We didn't know there was a crazy man hidden inside," said the youngest one. "We're sorry."

When the chief heard what had happened, he found another hiding place for Gouama. This time, he hid Gouama in an old oven with smoked fish stacked on top.

That night, the chief assembled the village to discuss what to do about their guests. A collection of smoked fish was gathered to sustain Sanou and his companion for their journey. The council of elders also decided to send two young men with them, until they arrived safely at the village where Diallo and his group awaited. At that point, the responsibility of the chief to his guests would be fulfilled.

Early in the morning, Gouama was called out from his oven. The moon had just completed its tour of the sky, and the stars had began to lose their luster. The cries of roosters could be heard throughout the village.

The chief hoped to inspire them for their journey with words of wisdom. As he spoke, however, his eyes were fixed upon Gouama: *"A man must understand his destiny and then bravely confront it,"* he said. *"The tool that he carries in his shorts is a symbol of this duty."*

The village still slept. A billy goat chasing a she-goat momentarily made Gouama's heart flutter, but he grew calm again and silently followed the others to the river's edge.

Before he climbed into the pirogue, the chief spoke to Gouama for a long time, reminding him of his duty as a man. *"A man must fight as long as a single breath remains within him. No situation is completely without hope. One must always fight. Always."*

Two pirogues glided over the surface of the calm water. One of the oarsmen began to sing. The morning breeze purified the echo of his voice, which harmonized with the sounds of nature.

Gouama clutched tightly onto the sides of the pirogue, which remained steady in the water. He relaxed at last and even admired the reflection of the moon across the water. "It's quite beautiful here," he told himself. "Very beautiful indeed."

He reflected upon the words of the village chief. He really did want to fight back, to be courageous. Still, his heart constricted inside his chest, beating wildly at the slightest mishap. It seemed to Gouama that he had completely lost control of this organ. He *must* master his heart! But how?

The pirogues skirted the river until the village finally disappeared from sight. With each slap of the oars against the water, the shirtless men sang together in rhythm with the paddles. Their joviality restored Gouama's spirits. Everything about these young men suggested life. Their arms with rippling biceps, their huge chests with expanded pectoral muscles, their large, cracked feet, colored from the river water, all of this seemed to Gouama a symbol of life and vitality.

They guided the pirogue towards solid land and helped Gouama to descend. Gouama retied the knot of his belt, an old nylon cord that had once been used for fishing. Sanou smiled to watch Gouama fumble with the knot. The fishermen seemed to have instilled in Gouama the desire to fight and triumph.

Gouama was now several pounds lighter, but he felt determined. With his new beard, dirt covering him from head to feet, a shepherd's gourd slung over one shoulder, and a walking stick in hand, he seemed an altogether different man.

His companions saved him from the difficulty of carrying the trip's provisions. They also stopped from time to time so he could rest and drink a special potion made from the fruits of the baobab tree, a parting gift from the villagers.

That night, before they slept, Sanou massaged Gouama's legs and prepared for him more soup with smoked fish. Gouama slept with very few disturbances. But each time he awoke, the reality of his situation overcame him, filling him with dread: He was a deposed president, a virtual dead man! Once again, he could not prevent the tears from flowing down his cheeks: "If only I could drive these tears away!" he thought.

For the first time, it occurred to him that there was at least one good thing about his plight: his children were still alive. He remembered that they had been invited to a party at the Ambassador's house the night of the coup d'état. The Ambassador would not let them be massacred, just as he would not put up with the regime that had deposed him, his old friend the Ambassador.

The main thing was to get to Zakro. Once in Zakro, he could bring the situation under control. "I must get to Zakro!" he said aloud. "I must get to Zakro!"

After more than a week of walking, they finally arrived at the village where Diallo and his group were supposed to be waiting. They stopped just outside the village to make inquiries. One of two local fishermen told them that Diallo and the others were no longer at the village but had left a message for Sanou regarding their whereabouts, at a village some twenty kilometers away.

The two fishermen offered to help them find their companions, thus reuniting the two groups, by taking them up river. They could even get there tonight if they traveled by pinasse, avoiding the long walk. Gouama liked this idea. Diallo and his companions had become like brothers to him. He even felt light-hearted enough to joke about the situation.

Sanou assumed the role of guide. He knew the entire region very well and was even well-known as a great sorcerer. Because of this, he decided to change their itinerary to avoid even the small villages. The police and the gendarmes had no doubt left outposts in all the local villages. Certainly, Gouama was no longer easy to recognize: his beard, loosely worn straw sandals, his pot-belly now flat with ridges, his former haughty appearance more like that of a limping beggar, his sporty gentleman's dress traded for the rags of a peasant, all helped to create the perfect disguise.

They guessed it would take about a month to make it to the West, the home of Sanou. They walked only a little each day, sleeping a great deal and, above all, moving forward only after sending out a scout. "Better late than never," Diallo agreed.

Sanou led them forward across a field some twenty kilometers from his village. He had built three dwellings there for his family. One of Sanou's wives and three of his girls were already busy preparing a meal for them, upon their arrival.

The rainy season had already come to the region. Even if the police were nearby, Sanou reasoned, they would never suspect that this scraggly and bearded peasant was the deposed president, now wanted throughout Watinbow. From under his enormous hat, Gouama's face would be difficult to spot, until they made it to Sanou's family compound.

From a village radio, Gouama learned who were the members of the new government. At first, he couldn't understand who the radio broadcasts refered to when they spoke of the new president, "General Kodio." It took an entire day for Gouama to realize that they meant his old underling "Sergeant Kodio." This realization made him so furious he threw his hat on the ground, kicked over a termitary, and began battling with shrubs and bushes before he was stopped by Diallo and one of the other young men. He wouldn't eat for the rest of the journey, mumbling to himself and flaying his arms about like a mad stage actor. Gouama kept up like this until falling asleep from exhaustion late that evening.

Sanou explained to the others that this "General Kodio" was an enemy of Gouama's family, that Gouama's bizarre behavior was due to the many sufferings Gouama and his family had endured at the hands of Kodio. The group could only be patient until they reached Zakro where Sanou knew three professional smugglers who would get them across the border.

Each morning, the fugitives anxiously awaited the arrival of these "ferrymen." The days grew long, tedious, and unpleasant. The heat that comes before the stormy weather, followed by the cold winds, little by little wore on their nerves. To pass the time, Diallo found a pack of cards which they played during the dreariest part of the day.

One evening, Sanou returned from a short journey, having learned that the guides were expected within three days. "Three more days!" Gouama moaned. Several times he had already asked Sanou to guide them all himself, but each time the old sorcerer had categorically refused. In the village, Sanou was suspected of selling his services to "big-shots" in the nation's capital. In the past, many expensive cars had pulled up in front of his compound. His family had always told their neighbors that Sanou journeyed to Zakro during his frequent absences. This same alibi now worked against him, after the police had begun making inquiries in the village regarding Gouama's whereabouts. They must therefore be patient and await Sanou's guides. There was no other choice.

Shortly before the arrival of the "ferrymen," Gouama was stricken with a violent pain in his left thigh, which eventually paralyzed his entire leg. Sanou tried every remedy known to him but nothing seemed to help. Gouama's leg visibly changed color, turning blacker than his other leg.

Diallo's young men, who had become like sons in the eyes of Gouama, were obviously worried about the severe state of Gouama's health. One of the young men, Mamadou, seemed familiar with this kind of illness. Privately, he told Sanou the name of Gouama's malady and insisted that the sick man be taken to a health unit. It might be his only chance of survival.

Sanou immediately rejected the suggestion that they take Gouama to a health unit. Mamadou did know the name of certain medications capable of curing Gouama of his illness.

"Where did you learn such things?" Sanou asked him, sternly.

Mamadou did not respond. He merely repeated that Gouama would die if he did not receive treatment within three days.

Sanou panicked. How would they get such medications without taking Gouama to a health unit? Gouama burned with fever, his body soaked in sweat, yet he shivered from cold at the same time. His leg grew more swollen and black. The young men uniformly insisted that Sanou go to a health unit and seek the proper medications for Gouama. He must bribe the head orderly, which would require a great deal of money. Sanou did not have nearly enough. Diallo had only three thousand CFA, the wages given to him by Sanou.

Gouama listened in on these discussions from under the little shelter they had built for him. He realized it was quite possible he would die, all because he lacked a few dollars. All the while, he had millions of dollars tucked away in his Swiss bank accounts. His eyes watered once again. He had just enough energy to ask Sanou to travel to the health unit, to beg the head orderly, do anything to get these medicines: "Maybe the head orderly will be a reasonable man," he said. "Maybe he'll take pity on us."

But Diallo and Sanou would not budge. Without money, they knew they would not get a single aspirin from any health unit in Watinbow. They cited examples of pregnant women as well as children who had died in the arms of their parents, all because they lacked the necessary money to "open the medicine cabinets" of the health units.

Still, something had to be done. Mamadou asked Sanou if he knew of an herb, a specific leaf or some other plant that would bring on a rapid and deep sleep. Sanou affirmed it was easy enough to find such an herb in the bush.

Diallo and his friends pulled together their meager resources, a little over three thousand CFA, and asked Sanou to accompany them to the nearest health unit that very night. For the journey, they purchased a liter of wine, which they opened as a precaution to pour out a libation before recorking the bottle. It did not take long to reach the health unit, a great white house where an enormous petrol lamp, round like the moon, burned from the window. They walked through a long corridor before finding a man asleep on a cot. Sanou woke him up and asked him if he was the guardian of the health unit. The man growled like an animal, insulting and threatening them for waking him up. He calmed down, however, when Mamadou held out a 500 CFA note. The guardian clutched at the money and pointed towards a door before falling back asleep on his cot.

Sanou knocked timidly at the door. After a long moment of silence, he knocked again only louder. Mamadou finally banged on the door with his open fist.

An angry voice at last answered, "Who is it? Who's there?"

"It's about a sick man, Doctor."

"Bring the sick man tomorrow."

"It's very grave, Doctor. He may die."

"Then let him die, if he can't wait till tomorrow."

Mamadou pushed a portion of the remaining money under the door. A few moments later, they heard a sound like squeaky bed-springs before the door finally opened. Mamadou handed over more money and the liter of wine. The orderly accepted their presents with a smile and told them to come in. Mamadou explained Gouama's symptoms, as the head orderly drank the wine in silence. A woman lay on the bed next to him, apparently asleep. Once the bottle was nearly a third empty, he asked Mamadou what it was he wanted. While Mamadou explained again Gouama's illness, the orderly crawled back under the covers. "Catherine," he said, shaking the woman beside him. "What do you think they need?"

"Aspirin," said a groggy female voice.

"But they gave me a liter of good wine and some money for cigarettes. I'm afraid we must open the medicine cabinet for them."

"Hand me the wine bottle and wake up the hired help. Have him fetch some aspirin and primperan, so we can get back to sleep. If these people knew how to eat better, they wouldn't get sick so often. But they never listen to us. Give me the wine bottle, Gerard, and go wake up that imbecile who works for us."

The hired help came without being called. He had overheard them speaking of the wine. "Hey, chief," he said. "How 'bout a glass for me?"

"You can have a few swigs, no more." the woman said. "Then go and get some aspirin and primperan for these gentlemen. Bring back the keys when you're finished. No wait, just push the keys under the door."

"The crack is not wide enough, Madame Catherine."

"All right, keep them till tomorrow. I don't want to be bothered. It's not every night Gerard and I work the same shift. Close the door behind them, will you Gerard?"

Outside, they heard the door being doubly bolted. The sound of squeaking bedsprings once again echoed from inside the chamber. The hired help put his ear against the door and lewdly licked his lips. "Okay," he said at last, "Follow me. I'll get you your... Your... Whatever it was that she said." He yawned widely. At first he could not get the key to turn in the door of the medicine cabinet. It was Mamadou who finally got the door open, calmly removing the necessary medications and then locking the cabinet back up. Before long, they were headed back to the sick man, giddy at their good fortune.

They found Diallo seated at the bedside of Gouama, who was now incapable of responding to their questions. His face was bathed in sweat and distorted from his illness. Mamadou gave him more than five injections before there was any marked improvement. Sanou also helped hold Gouama's mouth open so they could get the medicine down.

"Where did you learn to do these things, my son?" he asked Mamadou.

"I was once an orderly at a health unit. I simply watched what the doctors did and found that I could do them myself."

The next day Gouama's fever dropped, and his leg dramatically changed color. As consciousness returned, Gouama's first thought was that they had found a doctor to care for him. When he could speak, he asked Sanou how much all this had cost, bringing him a doctor? Wouldn't the doctor give away the secret of his identity? He smiled, shaking his head, when Sanou told him of the exploits of Mamadou and his companions. "You will all be richly rewarded when the time comes," he swore. "You will not regret it!"

After a week of treatment, Gouama could lift himself up and take a few steps. His healer ordered walking exercises and soon Gouama found his health returning. He called Mamadou "the man who made problems for others" after Sanou returned to the village with the health unit and learned that the orderly and his lover Catherine, another orderly, had slept through until the next morning on account of the wine. When the woman's husband came for her on his motor bike the next morning, he had found her nude upon the bed, sleeping in the arms of her lover. He seized a knife that lay on the table, cut off the ears of his rival, and made two large gashes on his cheeks. The orderly, who was completely nude, screamed and shot out of the health unit like a ball from a canon. The cuckolded husband tossed the ears in a bowl of rice and sauce that the hired hand had just prepared.

In the scandal that ensued, no one seemed to notice the stolen medications. Rumor had it that the woman had simply worn out her lover that night, causing them both to oversleep.

CHAPTER EIGHT

Now healed, Gouama helped Sanou and the others to till the soil and sow seedlings on Sanou's land. Each day, Gouama grew more gay, more confident in the future. They had missed the "ferrymen" because of Gouama's illness, but these guides were expected to return soon. From time to time, Gouama listened to the radio and heard the names of those responsible for his fall. Then Gouama would pace about grumbling under his breath. Before long, his anger would pass and he would again joke and banter with his companions. He even became something of a storyteller himself, recounting tales of past festivals, meetings, and travels. One day, when he was feeling particularly well, he began to speak of a meeting of African heads-of-state. He at once became aware of his mistake and quickly changed the subject.

The guides returned one night and a day for their departure was set. Gouama was jubilant. He even danced about when the radio played one of his favorite songs. His joy was short lived: the radio broadcast was interrupted to announce a speech by the new president, General Kodio. The blood rushed to Gouama's face. To hide his bad mood from the others, he sat off by himself and covered his eyes with his hand.

One of the guides spoke of a festival that the government had organized in the next day or so. Gouama jumped into the conversation at once. What was the exact date, he wanted to know? The rainy season having returned, the celebration of independence would not be far away, only he had lost track of the days. He remembered that in the early days of decolonization, the dates for celebrations were always carefully chosen to displace traditional festivals in favor of new ones.

Those who loved to drink and dance would be psychologically thrown off balance if the usual period of celebrations was passed over and new dates were selected instead. This advice was given to him and other African presidents by foreign experts: "Take stock of the feelings and sensibility of your subjects. Never forget that 'the black man is emotional while the white man is rational.' Remember this when you organize public festivals," Marcel had said to Gouama.

Certain new celebrations therefore intentionally undermined others, usually the traditional ones.

The national anthem could be heard on the radio. Gouama longed to cover his ears, but he could not resist listening to the speech. He would get even with this bastard Kodio later. "I will have his head on a platter," Gouama swore to himself.

"My dear compatriots," Kodio began. "As has been our tradition for many years, we will celebrate tomorrow the independence of our great nation. But this year, we have even greater reason to celebrate than in previous years. We must pause now to reflect upon the past, present, and future of our beautiful country.

"After a decade of independence, our situation is far from enviable. Ten years of fraudulence and fumbling by past leaders have left our country with a ball and chain attached. Instead of developing our country, Gouama and his helpers have plunged us deeper into debt and misery.

"Ten years. Ten long years. Nothing in the eyes of eternity, perhaps, but an eternity in the life of our people. For it takes only one year, one month, one day, or even one hour for an irresponsible leader to condemn his people to many years of slavery and misery, to the loss of their sovereignty.

"Ten years have passed since the colonial powers gave us, along with many other African nations, our independence. Despite their long subjugation, African peoples at last regained their liberty and even peace. The politicians of the past inspired us with dreams. They instilled hope in us before we awoke to find ourselves betrayed. We discovered that all our hard work was performed so that a handful of immoral men might rule over us like kings.

"For ten years, favoritism, nepotism, and corruption have been the order of the day, a way of life for our government officials. Meanwhile, the people have been hamstrung, their voices silenced, drowned out by those of a few spiteful men. Ten long years have passed while African people everywhere have worn themselves out applauding these notorious demagogues. For ten years, the destiny of our people has been in the hands of these irresponsible leaders, and in the hands of foreign outsiders. Virtual beggars on the international scene, these leaders spent enormous sums of money so they could travel about the world to vilify our people and barter our dignity for the sake of gaining foreign aid. This so-called aid has often been more of a nuisance than a help for our people.

"For ten hard years, they have tried to convince the people that independence meant extravagance, unnecessary luxuries for them and their coteries. It never occurred to any of these so-called leaders that independence might mean taking full responsibility for the destiny of our country.

"You know all of this, of course. You know very well the conditions under which your army was forced to assume power. You know very well the condition of your nation, as bequeathed to you by the deposed tyrant Gouama and his irresponsible cohorts, these men who plunged our country into its present misery. You know very well about the misdeeds of the old ruling party in our country.

"Why, may I ask, was this ruling party first created? After the second world war, those who constituted the African elite at that time, in other words, those who had the good fortune to be able to read and write, felt a tremendous hatred for our former colonizers. Such hatred was normal and justified, we told ourselves. But the true source of this hatred has rarely been brought to light. What these elite few really hated was their own impotence, their own failures to advance within the colonialist government. They were envious men, and they were rarely taken seriously by the colonialist bourgeoisie. So these men bided their time and waited for their revenge. They hated the colonizers for all the wrong reasons, out of pride, out of petty personal conflicts. They hated the colonizers because they themselves longed to lord over their own people as kings, to make slaves of their own people.

"What proof do we have of this, you may ask? The proof is evident in their manner of ruling, like absolute despots, after independence. The proof is evident in their willingness to indulge every personal whim and moral weakness, their inexcusable opulence, while their own people lived in utter misery and poverty. The proof is evident in their inability to unite the African continent. Far worse, the proof is evident in their inability to unite even their own countries.

"Where does the idea of a 'United States of Africa' come from? Casablanca, Monrovia, Addis-Ababa: a three-way chess match. Their organizations and summits have been still-born from the start.

"They have created their political parties, enlisting the support of their young people, all to gain empty applause. Such parties have always been the private property of a few elite men, men without shame who have ruthlessly exploited their people. These old parties sought to gain a certain credibility by way of international alliances that were bankrupt from the beginning."

At this point, Gouama was no longer able to control himself. He ran up to the radio, cursing and angrily waving his arms about. "The liar!" he shouted. "The son of a bitch!

Filthy..."

Diallo forcibly contained Gouama and led him far from the group, which sat listening to the radio transmission.

"Mister X was the leader of the leaders of Party A," the voice of Kodio continued. "Mister Y was the leader of the leaders of Party B. The conflicts between Parties A and B, and those leaders who jockeyed for position within these parties, were the only true struggles taking place, struggles for political power that left the African people out in the cold. These petty grudges and struggles for position are the true reasons for the lack of unity among African people today.

"All these political types suffer from delusions of grandeur and from superiority complexes. Such leaders believe themselves to be more intelligent than everyone else because they hold a university degree, a doctorate perhaps. At the university, such leaders learned that the only capable leaders are those with advanced diplomas. The valor of these men amounted to little more than a few empty and pompous words, spiced up with a little Latin. Political speeches for these people were like a kind of rosary of catch words and phrases with no bearing on reality. Whenever the tyrant Gouama gave a speech, it required a diploma just to sort through his pompous phrases and slogans, to get at his real meaning.

"Certain numbers of these people were arrogant about their power because they had once lived and worked among the former colonizers. *"Those who have worked and ruled with the whites,"* the people told themselves, *"will have no problem governing us and leading our country to prosperity."*

"This kind of logic justified the establishment of corrupt political parties and their leaders. And this is why we must banish and bury all those who helped empower these people, who created the conditions that led to their misdeeds. We must destroy everything; we must utterly crush the slightest remnants of these people and their corrupt government. We must begin again at ground zero. It is a difficult but noble task that awaits us. Henceforth, we will move forward, not back-wards. All that does not move forward invariably atrophies. On the question of development, it is impossible to stand still.

"Our coming into power now will detonate an explosion of liberty in Watinbow! Economic, political, and cultural prosperity will be within the reach of every loyal citizen!

"We invite all of you to walk this path with us, the path of patriotism that will lead to a new society, a strong and united nation! The future of Watinbow is up to all of us. We will all gain in peace and justice if we work together. But we must be wary of the vendors of ideology, the charlatans who offer us empty words and phantoms. We must not tolerate the anarchists among us.

"My dear compatriots, the way is paved for our freedom, for economic prosperity. Be confident in your army. It will not fail you.

"Long live the people! Long life Watinbow!"

The national anthem began to play once more over the radio. "Dear listeners," a voice soon could be heard, "we are going to switch now to a press conference with our Liberator, the Clairvoyant Witness for the People, our own national president, Etienne Kodio. This press conference was held earlier in the day with national and international reporters in attendance."

"To begin, Mr. President, why have you assumed power in Watinbow?"

"For numerous reasons. And, all the inhabitants of Watinbow know them: economic stagnation, the scandalous mismanagement of our common welfare, corruption, nepotism, and too many other ills to list here. But above all, to liberate my people from barbarism and tyranny. How many people have been killed in this country, imprisoned, or forced into exile during the ten year reign of Gouama? The numbers are countless. In such conditions, is it right that the Army should sit passively by? While citizens of Watinbow are being murdered and stolen from? While the country is being destroyed? I don't think so.

"And you forget one thing. In Africa, is there any other means of riding a people of a tyrant? The vote has proven useless with despots like Gouama."

"After the political prisoners from the former regime were liberated, there were some shocking discoveries, Mr. President. Why did the old regime choose to kill students and those prisoners suspected of being Marxists?"

"According to one wounded student we were able to save, the tyrant Gouama had a personal hand in this. Before fleeing Watinbow, he personally ordered the execution of all those suspected of being Marxists. Our men arrived too late to stop the slaughter."

"Where is the deposed president now?"

"All that we know is he is no longer in Watinbow. We know that he's amassed a large fortune in foreign bank accounts. It would not surprise anyone if he were to reappear one day at the head of an army of mercenaries. If he comes, you can be sure of one thing, we'll be ready for him."

"Was there due legal process that took place following the coup d'état? Were those who are now accused of crimes among your former political opponents?"

"Not in the least. After the murder of our brave commandants Ouedraogo and Keita, a murder that was staged by Gouama as an accident, we began a formal inquiry to shed light upon these great losses. The farcical inquiry ordered by the assassin Gouama has of course yielded nothing. But we have discovered that the closest collaborators in these odious murders were once great friends of the victims. The military tribunal overseeing this matter has been without pity for all those implicated in this abominable crime."

"Do you plan on making significant changes in the country's foreign policy?"

"We will remain faithful to all of our country's previous

obligations to the outside world. We look forward to working for peace and justice with all neighboring countries, at least those who respect our sovereignty. We will also take a close look at all accords drawn up between us and the West. We're guessing we may have to revise some aspects of these agreements."

"A last question, Mr. President. It is said that in Africa, when military men take power, they nearly always find some way of making sure it stays in their own hands: Through a single party state, through appointing themselves as presidents for life, and so on. Can we expect in Watinbow the emergence of a civil government in the coming months?"

"To begin, I think it's important to acknowledge that not all military regimes are the same. It is therefore misleading to generalize in this way. To speak of a civil regime as necessarily being in opposition to a military regime is to ignore certain realities in our country. What we'd like to do is tear down such artificial barriers, like those between civilians and military personnel. We will succeed in doing this.

"But whatever the specific situation may be, if we think we can merely copy Western models of democracy, especially at the current historical juncture, we will inevitably fail. Western style democracies are a luxury we Africans cannot afford. The people of Watinbow will wield the power, as we've promised. This is all we can say at the moment. If you had been present at the popular celebrations following the coup, I don't think you'd even ask such a question."

The familiar voice of the radio broadcaster announced the conclusion of the press conference: "Dear Listeners," he said. "We will now read to you a number of telegrams of support sent to the Savior of the People, the Liberator, the Messiah sent to us by God...."

"Turn off that radio! Turn it off or I'll smash it to pieces!" Gouama shouted. He sobbed, holding a club in one hand. Gouama's sobs racked his body, like those of a professional mourner at a public funeral. Everyone stopped talking so they could better hear his sobs. Passersby were indignant until Sanou explained the reasons for the hatred of this man they called the "womanly man": *"It's an old family grudge,"* Sanou said, shrugging his shoulders.

CHAPTER NINE

The next day, at an early hour, the three "ferrymen" were all so well hidden in the surrounding bush that only Sanou was able to spot them as they emerged from the trail leading to the river. Gouama remained silent, as he had ever since the speech and press conference of the new president. After his outburst, no one had spoken a word to him. In transit, however, when a thorny branch pricked him in the shoulder, he grew enraged as if personally attacked. He grabbed hold of the branch and hurled it in a clump of bushes, only to find himself ensnared in more thorns. The entire group of travelers burst into laughter. They had to use machetes to cut him out. Afterwards, Gouama stripped the thorn branch and used it to clean his teeth.

After five days of walking, the ferrymen arranged a halt before noon, at the edge of a river. "On the other side of this river is the territory of Zakro," said one of the guides.

Gouama applauded until his hands were sore.

"You'll wait here until we find out the market dates of the local villages along the border. If we want to get through unobserved, we must travel by bush taxi, one that is heading for a local market."

"But I don't want to evade the police," Gouama said. "In fact, I want to contact the police as soon as possible."

"You'll wait here like all the others. You will be free to sort out your personal problems in due time." Having said that, the three ferrymen rowed across the river.

Diallo begin preparing the meal. Gouama called Mamadou and his friends under a tree. "I would like to speak to you," he said. "You saved my life, you even risked your own lives to help me. In our days, such a thing is very rare, almost unheard of. I would like to reward you, to richly reward you. Until now, I have hidden my identity, but I am the president of the country, of Watinbow. I am fleeing from those who have usurped my rightful place. When I arrive in Zakro, I will organize an army to punish these thieves, these traitors.

"Once I am restored to power, I will appoint all of you to very important posts in our country. But in the meantime, I will give each of you a large sum of money. This will be a gift, not a loan. I'd like each one of you to name a figure, an amount of money that would make you happy."

Gouama looked first at Mamadou and then his companions. Their faces, however, revealed nothing, no reaction at all. "You have nothing to say?" Gouama asked.

"What is it you want us to say? We are not traveling to the same places. Our paths are different. After Zakro, we will travel on to Watinoma. And we cannot realistically wait around while you beg for money to give us."

"Beg for money! I don't have any intention of begging for money. I *have* money, lots of it! I have money in Switzerland. I'll simply go and get my money."

"What will the authorities of Zakro say?"

Gouama laughed in a haughty voice and spoke with great assurance. "President Dagny is an old friend of mine. I will be received with all the honors due to a neighboring president. President Dagny and I have fought together and have won great victories together. He will help me gain the support of the Western nations to crush these petty soldiers."

"We have little confidence in African princes, Mr. Gouama. It seems to us that you may be in for an unpleasant surprise."

"But you understand nothing, Mamadou! Listen to me.

Dagny and I are old, old friends. We have sworn fidelity to one another, should a coup ever take place. We've even shared the same bedroom. When I recently visited Zakro, for example, he supplied me with seven young girls in seven nights, everyone of them beautiful virgins. I've done the same for Dagny when he came to Watinbow.

"We have accounts in the same banks. Dagny even bought one of my castles in Normandy, to help me out when I was cash-strapped."

"A bourgeois never has a friend who is not also a member of the bourgeoisie. His only morality is the preservation of his private property. If your friend Dagny finds that you are still..."

"Listen, Mamadou," said Gouama, interrupting, "I don't like these school boy words in your mouth. What does it mean to be 'bourgeois'? To be a member of the 'bourgeoisie'? It's all nonsense."

"In Africa, the bourgeois are those who drive a Mercedez rather than ride on the back of a donkey," Mamadou said, "those who never drink millet beer or palm wine, except during big celebrations, those who drink champagne to celebrate, those who live on caviar and camembert, on grilled steaks instead of rice with sauce, those who carry about suitcases filled with clothes, instead of running around naked until their tenth birthdays. The bourgeoisie are those who have forgotten what it means to be poor, who have forgotten the misery of their people. These people are the bourgeoisie."

Gouama stared at Mamadou with his mouth agape. He could only shake his head. "You hold it against a man because he drives a Mercedez instead of riding on a donkey's back? Because he brings real progress to his native land? My child, you are confused."

"It is not I who am confused. It is those who have forgotten the misery of their people who are confused." Mamadou said. "It is hardly a question of progress that a few Africans now drive about in a Mercedez. This seems funny to me, that you would call such a thing 'progress.' There are those like me who are skeptical of such progress, who do not look upon the new buildings in the capital, the streets that have been paved, or the factories built as 'progress.' There are many like me who doubt such 'progress,' who do not believe that the rise of the military in our country with its multitude of generals, colonels, and other officers is truly 'progress' for us. If Africa has 'progressed,' why is there no food for the poor? Why hasn't agricultural production increased? It seems to me that the only thing that has 'progressed' has been Africa's foreign debt. No wait, the number of coup d'états has also 'progressed,' I suppose."

"You surprise me, Mamadou! You speak like some kind of Marxist student, envious of the prosperity of others. If by chance you happened to have heard the diatribes of one of these malcontents and were seduced by such claptrap, it's high time you woke up and began seeing things as they really are. These students are all working for foreign governments, don't you know that? For bloodthirsty Marxists who thrive on violence. Mamadou, you and your friends are different. You are exceptional young men, men with noble hearts, men who are well loved by God..."

"That's enough. Look, in Africa, everything comes from the outside. The workers protest against the inhuman treatment they suffer, but it's precisely foreign strangers who are most responsible for their exploitation. These students you despise merely dare to try and understand the sufferings of the people. They're not working for strangers. They're trying to figure out what strangers have done to us. Think about it. Do you really need a stranger to tell you that things are going badly? Do you have to read Lenin to grasp the fact that that you don't have a job? Do you have to read Marx to understand that you're hungry and thirsty?

"Is it necessary to study the Bolshevik or Chinese revolutions to understand that it is those societies where corruption, nepotism, and tribalism flourish that are rotten, that are the actual cause of violence, hatred, and crime among the people? Do you need to study such things in school to worry that your country may slide into complete anarchy? To worry about what may happen to the people you love, should your country fall apart?

"I can't imagine a more dangerous villain in our country than a corrupt leader. Even a murderer can only inflict limited damage, before he is finally caught, but a tyrant who ruthlessly exploits his people inflicts immeasurable damage. I can't really imagine a more serious enemy of the people than a tribalist who disguises himself as a businessman. I'm sorry, Gouama, but it seems to me that your so-called 'morality,' your great 'wisdom,' and political expertise amount to little more than a kind of varnish to gloss over the horrible crimes you have committed. The fact is, you don't fool anybody. It's been a long time since you fooled anybody."

"You insult me now, Mamadou."

"Take if for an insult, if you like. We probably should have left you to die since it's your regime which has corrupted our country."

"It's not me who instructed the people to steal and be corrupt! How many times in my speeches did I speak out against these plagues on our society?"

"It's true that many times you said such things, but did you really believe them yourself? What example did you set for the people when you were in power? These evils that you denounced were the inevitable consequences of your own regime."

"With me as president, we had a liberal, open political system."

"Just like the United States and Europe, only in the lawless domain of the economic, not in our political system. There can be no real economic freedom without political freedom in equal measure. Think about it, Gouama. Out here in the bush, a man does what he says he's going to do. It's the same for all of us. But if you presume to guide the destiny of others, you must be willing to sacrifice your own destiny, your own personal desires. If you prevent others from speaking freely about their deepest hopes and dreams for the future, you inevitably prolong their underdevelopment."

"You're really going to refuse my offer? Do I understand you correctly?"

"I don't think I can be any clearer. Not only do we refuse your offer, we ask you now to give back everything you have stolen from the people of Watinbow. Go ahead, go to Europe. But once you're there, use your money to build schools and hospitals in Watinbow. You could do it through some charitable intermediary. The Ambassador, for example. No doubt you'd be well received at the Ambassador's house. That way he could use you to frighten Kodio from time to time. The tradition of granting hospitality to foreign despots in the Ambassador's country assures you of a comfortable exile."

"You're crazy, Mamadou. You're really refusing the chance I'm offering you? Look, if you decide to stay in Zakro, my offer still stands. I'll always help you if you need it."

"We will not stay in Zakro. We already told you where we're headed. So let me give you a few words of advice. This international mafia that you've organized along with the president of Zakro, and that you pompously call an "open alliance," only had meaning so long as you were still president of Watinbow. Watch out, Mr. Gouama."

Gouama burst into laugher. "Thanks for the advice, Mamadou. Thank you very much. I will certainly keep it in mind. But tell me now, and speak frankly, who are you anyway? It's clear you're no simple peasant."

"Since you've asked, I'm happy to tell you. My name is Coulibaly, general secretary of the student movement in Watinbow and fifth year medical student. I'm an old prisoner of yours. My two companions are also students, both members of the student movement and former prisoners, *your* prisoners. We're here because we were sentenced to death by the coup-makers. We barely escaped from them the night of the coup. We were kept in a cell a little ways off from the cell with the other students. That's how we were able to escape. They lined up all those accused of being Marxists against the wall of our cell and mowed them down with machine guns. One of the guns accidentally shot off the lock of our cell. That's the only reason we're still alive and could take care of your phlebitis.

"We knew very well who your were before you became ill. In fact, we risked our lives to save you precisely because of who you are. Not that we wouldn't have done the same for someone else, only we were particularly inspired in your case. We wanted to relish our victory. You condemned us to death, and it was us who saved your life.

"Africa, *our* Africa, will win in the end. The people will triumph. And one day, the people will humiliate you and all those like you, just as we have humiliated you today. History will march forward. Gouama and those like him cannot stop the course of history. Adieu!"

Gouama stood utterly baffled. He could not believe his ears. He stammered out a few incoherent words of apology, but Mamadou and his friends had already left. They now stood by Diallo, who was busy preparing the food.

Gouama himself did not eat for the rest of the day. His silence grew even more profound. He remained utterly mute until they took their first footsteps in the Republic of Zakro. Finally, he spoke to Diallo. "I would like you to do me a favor," he said. "Could you speak on my behalf to your brothers? I'm fully aware of the harm that I have done them. I'm prepared to offer them millions, so they can began their lives anew. Please speak to them. Try to convince them to accept my gift. They saved my life in spite of the terrible things I did to them. They have taught me a lesson, and I'm truly sorry. Tell them I am beginning to understand the absurdity of my previous views about Marxism. Tell them, please. Above all, you must make them accept something from me, some token of my gratitude."

"It's useless, Mr. Gouama. I know them all very well. Even if they were dying of starvation, they would never accept money from you. But if it's true that you feel you've learned something, teach those like yourself. Teach all those who label others 'Marxists' and 'revolutionaries' what harm such words do, how they needlessly divide African peoples and distract them from the real battles that confront us. The true battle in Africa is not between pseudo- 'moderates' and pseudo- 'progressives' but between the exploiters and the exploited, the rapists and those who are raped. Teach all those you know. Tell it to Dagny in Zakro and those like him.

"Mister Gouama, let Coulibaly and his friends go in peace. You have been saved. You will soon be in possession of your millions and be reunited with your friends. That's enough good luck for one man. But there is one last thing I must also say to you: There is no real happiness for anyone unless there is happiness for everyone, for all of the people."

"Diallo, I would like to give you a few million because you also saved my life. Please, do not refuse me. You could buy a great herd of cattle with my gift."

"The cattle that I have are enough, Mister Gouama. I inherited my herd from my grandfather, who worked like a slave to keep them together. As soon as I got out of prison, I returned to my parents, who are cattle-herders like me. I returned to a hard life of toil, but it has its advantages and pleasures."

"You were in prison too? Because... because of me?"

"Yes, of course. After I returned from France, where I was seeking my university diploma. There wasn't a university for me in Watinbow because, like many other African leaders, you choose to build prisons rather than schools. When I made my first voyage home from France, I was accused of trafficking in dope. The tribunal sentenced me to seven years in prison. The real reason was that I was suspected of being a Marxist, a subversive. I am the famous Diallo of Feyssart. The others came to me because they needed a place to hide out, after they escaped from prison.

"Adieu, Mr. Gouama. Above all, do not forget the words we have spoken to you today. The biggest error any man can make in our days is to fail to understand the aspirations of his society, of his people. In other words, to ignore history itself."

CHAPTER TEN

Sanou gave his remaining money to the ferrymen so they could buy new clothes for Gouama. Gouama was thus able to barter off his peasant clothes for a reasonably new outfit, although he was forced to wear slippers instead of shoes. Walking about the market with Sanou, he regarded the merchants with a haughty air, especially irritated at the hours wasted merely to save a few pennies. The chaotic activity in the marketplace did not, however, disturb his daydreams very deeply. He spoke aloud to himself, dramatically waving one finger, as if arguing with someone. Only a few children took notice of the new "madman" in the marketplace.

In the late afternoon, the bush-taxi chauffeur began to load their baggage. The ferrymen had been paid to take them as far as Aty, two hundred kilometers away from the border. Their work was accomplished. Aty was the biggest village along the border of Zakro. Once the seventy passengers were packed into the old Izuzu bus with Gouama and the others, the driver stowed the enormous slab of wood that served as a tire jack upon the roof of the vehicle. The bus now rushed down a steep road, backfiring three times before its engine smoothly hummed, leaving behind a thick cloud of black smoke. A concert of bleatings and cries from the sheep and goats who were tied to the roof broke the stillness of the evening.

After what seemed like endless hours on the road, the drive interrupted several times to attend to mechanical breakdowns,

Gouama and the other passengers arrived at Aty after two in the morning. Stiff from the ride, Gouama climbed out of the bus and asked for directions to the police station. It wasn't more than five meters from where he stood. He whistled softly to himself, his hands in his pockets. At the police station, he found two officers snoring on their mats.

"What is it?" one of them said gruffly. "What do you want?"

"I'd like to speak with someone. The person in charge here."

"Come back in the morning."

"You mean that..."

"Is it an emergency of some sort?"

"Yes and no."

"All right, since you can't make up your mind, why don't you hit the road?"

"I am the former president of Watinbow, President Gouama. I just arrived in Zakro and..."

"Sergeant, shut this idiot up. We'll deal with him in the morning."

"Please, I only..."

"You only what? All right, if you insist, come in and sleep on the floor. We'll worry about it tomorrow."

Gouama timidly entered the station bureau where the two officers reclined on their mats. One of the officers unfurled a mat for him on the floor. "Sleep here till morning, chief. Otherwise, you'll be in big trouble. You're only a president, see, but I'm an Ayatollah."

"Sergeant, it looks like we have a new mad-man on our hands. He just got off the bush-taxi."

The morning seemed like it would never come. Gouama did not sleep a wink. The strong stench of the police station was unbearable. Once, after the two officers had fallen back asleep, Gouama went outside and vomited. When morning came, the guards told the relief duty that Gouama was a mad-man who believed he was a president. Gouama asked if he could speak with their superior officer but was refused. He was beginning to grow angry and now addressed them in a threatening voice: "You're making a very serious mistake, a mistake that will cost you dearly. President Dagny and I will make sure every one of you lose your jobs. I'm a friend of his. I am the former president of Watinbow."

The guards exploded in laughter. Gouama now became enraged. He beat his hands against the metal door and began to shout insults. The noise made by the door drew out the police commissioner from the back room.

"What's all this racket?" he said. He stared evenly at Gouma, smoking a cigarette.

"It's a madman, sir."

"I am not a madman," Gouama said. "I asked to speak with you and they refused me."

"What is it you want?"

"I am the former president of Watinbow, a personal friend of..."

"You already told us that. What is it you want?"

"I want you to inform President Dagny of my presence here."

"That's all you want?" the commissioner laughed to himself.

"Tell him that I have suffered a great deal, that I'll be in need of medical attention. His phone number is 33-28-44-57."

The commissioner stopped laughing. "Repeat that number," he said.

"With pleasure: 33-28-44-57."

The commissioner's cigarette fell from his mouth. "Bring him in here," he said, when he could speak. "Place armed guards outside the door."

Around noon, a helicopter descended from the village, not far from the police station. A national security officer disembarked from the helicopter. After a brief interview with

Gouama, the two men climbed into the helicopter, which rose high in the sky, as the mortified police commissioner and his guards looked on.

CHAPTER ELEVEN

Gouama was received by Zakro's Minister of the Interior. A villa and numerous employees were allocated to him, as well as a fully furnished wardrobe. Shaven and fresh, Gouama strolled about the garden of the villa, his face radiant two days after his arrival. President Dagny was out of the country, he was told, and not expected for several days. Gouama asked to speak with him over the telephone, but the Minister of the Interior refused him. President Dagny had expressly forbidden that he be contacted, unless it was an urgent matter of national security.

Instead Gouama was invited to dine at the home of the Minister of the Interior. Over dinner, Gouama improvised a speech that magnified the good relations between his country and Zakro, as well as President Dagny's wisdom, clairvoyance, and courage. Gouama felt very well by the end of the meal, after renewing his acquaintance with fine wine and gourmet cuisine. "This is how life is meant to be lived!" he told himself.

Within a week, Gouama received many of Zakro's grand personages in his villa and was in turn received by them. Everyone deplored his premature fall from office. Everyone praised the steps he had taken to save Watinbow from underdevelopment, to modernize his impoverished nation. Everyone cursed the rise of military regimes in harsh, unequivocal terms. Above all, everyone promised him undying support and assistance to help him save the country he had built up with his own hands. Nothing lacked to add to Gouama's happiness, except his throne. He already felt as if he was restored to power.

Gouama had established contact with a "great man" in the import-export business based in Watinoma. He asked him for news of Tiga, but there was no trace of his special advisor. However, after several more attempts to establish contact, Gouama learned that Tiga had liquidated all of his holdings in Watinbow, amassing a large fortune and fleeing to Nigeria in the company of a young woman. The brother of the young woman gave him the phone number of his new "brother-in-law." Gouama rang the number several times, but without success. On the other end of the line, he was told that the "boss" of a firm called "Frutexport" was away on a business trip. Losing patience, Gouama exploded in rage. "Tell him that if he doesn't call me here tomorrow, I will not call him again. If that happens, he himself will be responsible, not me! You got that? He'll be completely responsible for what happens to him!"

Gouama waited nervously, but Tiga never returned his call. His business in Nigeria was flourishing. In fact, when Tiga learned of Gouama's threats, he laughed until the tears rolled down his cheeks. Even if Gouama returned to power, he had nothing to fear. He had prepared for this eventuality for more than six years, when he had first gotten involved in exporting gold, diamonds, and drugs. Each time Gouama had made a trip to Europe or America, Tiga had always profited from the occasion by exporting one thing or another. In two short years, he had become a millionaire. As things stood now, there was little that worried him. Tiga was dead. He was now El Hadjj Moussa Alassane, born in Kaduna, Nigeria of parents who were extremely rich. His family in Watinbow would join up with him, once things quieted down. Life in a third world country certainly has its ups and downs, he loved to repeat.

After the brief period of Tiga's disgrace had passed, the new authorities of Watinbow would be embroiled in dealing with the public's discontent over their poverty, misery, and unemployment. At that time, he could even return to Watinbow to make an investment or two. With all the unemployment, he would no doubt be well received. And who could say what might happen after that? He could become an important business partner to the new strong men in Watinbow. Conducting business and dealing with easy and rapid wealth are the childhood illnesses of new third world regimes, he assured himself.

CHAPTER TWELVE

The Minister of the Interior of Zakro had drawn up with Gouama a proposal to submit to President Dagny. However, Dagny had expressly forbidden Gouama to meet with certain people: diplomats and those who were involved in Watinbow organizations that were based in Zakro. They had to be discrete, very discrete, he said. Gouama had no choice but to defer. But one evening, after the Minister of the Interior had kept him waiting until almost midnight, Gouama at last lost all patience. With rage in his heart, he directly confronted the Minister, demanding to know what was going on.

"Mr. President," the minister said. "You must excuse me for keeping you so long."

Mr. President! That phrase alone helped to make him happy, momentarily restoring his peace of mind.

"Mr. President, I just received a message for you from your colleague President Dagny. He has read your proposal and is quite satisfied with it. But he asks for a few slight revisions. He feels strongly that you must first draw upon the support of the people of Watinbow to restore your power. Relying upon foreigners and mercenaries should be a last recourse, after all else fails. From Zakro, we have been able to establish contact with a number of military officers who remain loyal to you. This is where we must begin. According to my special agents, the demonstrations of military support were mostly staged by the coup-makers. Among the general population, there are many who are not happy with the coup. Many remain loyal to you."

"Excuse me for interrupting, my dear Minister, but we are dealing with a profoundly ungrateful people. How could they possibly applaud these thieves who have so viciously attacked their liberator?"

"You're absolutely right, Mr. President. African people are a profoundly ungrateful lot. Look at what's happened here in Zakro. President Dagny fought courageously against colonialism, which enabled our people to live in peace and freedom. But certain teachers who were virtual puppets of international Marxists begin spreading their lies in the high schools, universities, and the streets of Zakro. Instead of supporting President Dagny, those who live in the bigger cities did not hesitate to show their support for these vandals. The workers even wanted to go on strike to show their support for the student movement.

"What could be more ungrateful than a people who were once bullied, beaten, and slapped about, who are now free and fully independent, thanks to the efforts of Dagny, and who are today ready to turn a cold shoulder to their savior, due to the slightest difficulties?"

"I don't know, Mr. Minister," Gouama said. "They seem very ungrateful indeed. It's the same thing in my country. There is an economic recession everywhere right now: in the United States, in France, everywhere. Am I personally responsible for a global economic recession? The irresponsible even blame me for famine and drought, as if our underdevelopment is somehow my fault."

"We have closely followed your efforts to increase agricultural production. Stability is the greatest wealth that a president can offer his people. This is what you gave to Watinbow."

"You're quite right. Global inflation, international economic crisis, falling exchange rates, who doesn't deal with such problems today? And everyone wants a job! Everyone wants to get paid for their work instead of cultivating the earth!"

"The black man wants to have his cake and eat it too. He wants it all, right away and for himself alone. The people are illiterate, but they ask for mathematical figures and public talks, all so they can be convinced we really don't have oil wells like they do in the Persian Gulf. The people must try harder to understand that a president is not a magician with a magic wand who can wave away all their problems.

"In any event, Mr. Gouama, you can rely upon President Dagny and Zakro to help you. Zakro will be your base, the citadel from which you will launch your assault on these usurpers. We will therefore need funds to organize and figure out the best strategies for success. By order of President Dagny, I opened up a bank account for you in Zakro. As you know, President Dagny is one of your most faithful friends. But Zakro has had trouble raising cash lately. To speed things up, since I'm guessing you'll want your throne restored as soon as possible, you must draw upon your own financial resources."

"I'm in complete agreement. For the moment, I'd like nothing better than to get to Europe so I can begin putting my money in that bank account you've opened for me. I'll leave it to my friend and brother Dagny to convince my old and faithful friends in Europe and elsewhere of the necessity to offer me their support."

"Everything will be done according to your desires, Mr. President. Here is a passport in good order we've prepared for you. I'll buy the plane tickets tomorrow morning. In two days, our Minister of Foreign Affairs will accompany you wherever you'd like to go. When you return, we'll reflect upon the best lines of attack. I sincerely hope that you are restored to power, especially to correct some of your previous mistakes. For, I must tell you, it seems to us that you have made some grave miscalculations. The biggest mistake you made was to place too great a trust in your country's military."

"You needn't say another word. There will no longer be a single military camp in the capital, once I'm restored to power. I'll ship them all to the country's borders. Their meager gas rations won't even permit them to make it back to the capital. They'll be issued rifles without ammunition."

"When you are abroad," the Minister said, "you must travel with complete discretion. You must not meet with anyone in any potentially dangerous places. You understand, I'm sure, the need for discretion. Right now, there's no way of knowing who's for you and who's against you. This venture must not fail, not just for your sake but for ours as well. These military types need to be taught a lesson that will echo all over Africa. If I may, there is one further suggestion as well..."

"Go ahead, my dear Minister. Please, we should leave no stone unturned."

"I would suggest to you, your Excellency, that you hold nothing back from your private funds. You must spare no expense in regaining your power. Press every means at your disposal to win this battle. We will furnish you with guns and ammunition. But it will be important that you yourself be near at hand. Zakro will make an excellent base for you."

"I understand your meaning perfectly, my dear Minister. We will make a quick trip to Zurich and then Paris and come straight back to Zakro. I'd like to give you a list of business-men in my country for you to contact. I have every confidence in those I've listed."

"Be very careful, my dear President. You may risk another coup if you can't trust these men."

"There's no question about these men's loyalty. They are all relatives of mine. They still live in Watinbow."

"Do you have any other questions? Anything we can help you with? Are you satisfied with your cook?"

"She does a good job, but she's not my type. Her breasts show the marks of her lifestyle and profession. She can stay on as a cook, but I'd prefer something a little more tender, a choicer piece of ass, if you catch my meaning. Something befitting the dignity of a president."

"Tomorrow I'll send over five new girls for you to choose from. The rest we'll send back."

"Why not keep two or three on hand? Even all five? A man likes a little variety from time to time. With five, it'll be like old times for me, like it was back in my palace."

"Consider it done, Mr. President. Until tomorrow."

Gouama did not sleep all night. He kept thinking of what would happen after his fortune was transferred to Zakro. If it was necessary, he'd spend every single penny to oust the traitor Kodio and restore himself to power. How would he punish Kodio, he wondered? Maybe I'll cut off his penis and his tongue? No, I'll hang him by his feet with his legs spread, and every two minutes a drop of nitrious acid will drip into his open anus. Beforehand, I'll personally eat his ear, his fingers and toes, while he watches.

Gouama sat down to write out a list of names, the names of those men who would make up his new government. But who should he appoint? Perhaps it was better to wait and see? What he could do was develop a whole new strategy for governing. He must divert the people's attention away from political questions, outside of the party demonstrations he'd be certain to organize.

He recalled what one of his old European advisors had told him before signing off on his country's independence: "*If you don't want an adversarial people, there is only one solution: create a happy, joyous people. To make them happy, let them dance and drink. Above all, let them drink! You must adopt a politics of drinking. Encourage the building of breweries.*"

Why hadn't he paid more attention to this advice? After he returned to power, Gouama vowed to finance two brand new breweries in Watinbow, out of his own pocket if necessary.

Sports also could play an important role in development.

Marcel had never ceased urging him, "_Reorganize sports in your country. Spare no expense. You know how the people love sporting events. If the people are busy with sports, their minds won't be on politics. You will avoid untold troubles and political challenges._"

But what should he do about the Marxists? He thought of Mamadou and his friends, the young men who had saved his life. How could such gentle and likeable young people, who were so humane and kind to him, also be subversives and Marxists, he wondered? It didn't make any sense. Henceforth, he would not kill Marxists but instead create a camp for their re-education. Only those who earned an exit diploma would be allowed to return to live in society. I'll also do something for those fishermen too, he thought. I'll have to think of something that'll ease their struggles.

He sat down his pen and glanced through the pages of notes he had made so far. His notes seemed rather haphazard, random ideas that had popped into his head. Outside, the morning sun cast its pale light upon the trees and flowers in the garden of his villa. Birds gaily chirped to usher in the coming day. Gouama also found himself humming a tune from his school days, a song about a pretty bird who sang of courage, patriotism, and chivalry.

He turned on the little transistor radio that was given to him by the Minister of the Interior of Zakro. The radio broadcaster spoke of a horrible massacre perpetuated by a group of terrorists. He remembered a day when he was tilling the soil of Sanou's field with the others. He had wanted to debate the question of terrorism with Mamadou and his friends. However, Mamadou had quickly cut him off. "_The kind of terrorism you speak of doesn't interest us. It is the logical consequence of a society in which the political and economic bases are off kelter, in which the government in power systematically deceives its people._

"_The terrorism that interests us comes from London, Paris, and Washington. It is the terrorism of those who determine the value of our labor, of those who have never seen a coffee plant and yet fix the price_ *of coffee on the market. That is a form of terrorism worth thinking about. Those who get rich on our misery are the real terrorists, not those poor wretches you mentioned earlier. The terrorists who harm us live on Wall Street, in the business districts of Paris and London. Our enemy is the IMF. Our islamic jihad is against the World Bank."*

Gouama had wanted to argue with Mamadou but was afraid of blowing his cover. He wondered now how such a bright young man could be so narrow-minded? How could Mamadou so stubbornly ignore the global realities confronted by political leaders like himself? It was as if Mamadou wanted to reduce the economic problems of the entire world to the way they effected a single continent. Why was he unable to see the bigger picture?

Gouama was hungry now. Every since he'd arrived in Zakro, he'd had little time to sit down and eat. He stuffed himself every chance he got. He had had a close brush with death. He wanted to take advantage now of the good things in life. It wasn't long before he heard the footsteps of the servant who brought him his morning coffee. He noticed immediately that she wore a sheer dress, revealing a white slip from underneath.

"Have you seen the cook yet?" he asked her.

"Yes, sir."

"I told you to call me 'Mr. President,'" he said, irritably. "I'll let it go this once, but I hope you'll remember next time. Why don't you go freshen up in the bathroom? Then climb out of that dress and wait for me on my bed. If you're cold, you can crawl under the covers."

"Yes, sir," she said, "Mr. President..."

Later that day, Gouama was awoken from his troubled slumber by a ringing telephone. "President Gouama?" a voice said. "It's the Minister of the Interior. Your plane leaves tonight for Switzerland, Swissair, a Boeing 747."

"Perfect," said Gouama. "I'll be ready."

CHAPTER THIRTEEN

The airport. Gouama felt like a new man, a man of the world. The throng of travelers breathed new life into him. He felt completely revived. Decked out in a three-piece, navy blue suit, derby hat upon his head, and a cane in one hand, he walked the airport corridors like true royalty. This was the good life! Only the memory of Mamadou, which occasionally came to mind, dampened his high spirits. A good man, that Mamadou, but hasty in his judgment. How could he possibly doubt progress in Africa? You had to get a glimpse of America and Europe to appreciate true progress, and to realize just how far Africa had come since independence. If Mamadou could see the African women who lived in these places, with their chic dresses and manicured nails! Reflected in the lights of the giant airport, their glamorous faces could light a thousand and one fires. Their perfume, their jewelry, all indisputable signs of development and progress, the dormant potential of the African woman. How could Mamadou and his friends believe for a single instant that their country and their continent had not progressed, Gouama wondered?

"What did you say, Mr. President?"

"Excuse me, Mr. Minister, I was thinking aloud. I was recalling the words of a reckless fellow I know who dared to suggest that Africa had not really progressed since decolonization."

"No doubt a very *young* man, an imbecile like those who

pack our universities today."

"A Marxist," Gouama said.

"Just what I was going to say. Look around you at those you see here today. Even the clothes of these people demonstrate the progress our country has made."

"My sentiments exactly. These are wonderful people. It does one good to see them kissing their loved ones goodbye."

"They're quite fashionable, especially the pretty young women. You know, Mr. President, we must find a radical solution to deal with these Marxist devils. We'll speak more of this later. I think we're supposed to board our plane now."

Being in the airport reminded Gouama of happier days. This marvellous world of airports, the sound of jet engines, the voices over the loud speakers. There was only one thing missing: a drum concert and traditional dances to mark his departure. But that was a small detail, of little significance.

The heavy Boeing 747 of Swissair took flight like an enormous vulture that had just feasted on an elephant. Gouama settled into his seat and slept. He flew towards Switzerland. He flew towards power, *his* power. He saw himself walking through the great portals of History. The media would praise his great feat: "*Temporarily upset by a military coup d'etat, President Gouama has returned to power. The crowds are lined up outside the capital of Watinbow to show their enthusiasm and support for this illustrious statesman who brought independence to his country...*"

During the course of the great ballroom celebration that he would organize, he would recount to everyone stories of his flight to Zakro: How he engaged in combat with more than fifty soldiers before he realized he must abandon the fight. How he heroically traveled through the wilds of Watinbow, braving vicious beasts and serpents. How he crossed a treacherous, crocodile infested river. He could hear already the voices of the women who would sing his praises, of his valor and courage. Ah, the gentle sex! How they love heroes! And nobody's heroic exploits could compare with Gouama's. He

134

was shaken from his daydream by an airline stewardess who offered him breakfast. Gouama ordered a bottle of champagne. This was a flight worth celebrating! He glanced at his watch and took note of the date. Henceforth, this would be a day of national celebration in Watinbow. He would call it the Day of Victory.

He recalled the wise words of the old fisherman: "*No problem is insurmountable. Each problem has its own proper solution.*"

Glory was his. The heroes of Watinbow fly towards victory, towards the consecration of their finest hour!

"To your health, Miss," he said to the stewardess. "Drink to health of a happy man."

Gouama beamed with happiness. Those who sat near him watched him with amusement. The Minister who accompanied him implored him to calm down, but to no avail. Gouama's exuberance was without limits. He offered champagne to everyone in first class. "To your health!" he cried, moving from chair to chair, a champagne bottle in hand.

"What is the occasion?" he was asked. "Is it your birthday?"

"It's a day I'll never forget," he said, drunkenly. "Courage and audacity soar into the heavens tonight. They soar upon the wings of science. Power and hope triumph!" Gouama began to sing as those in first class applauded him. In his happiness, he even recited Ronsard's "Odes to Cassandra" with all the gestures of a professional actor. At last, his companion the Minister succeeded in getting him back in his seat.

The calm voice of the airline stewardess announced the plane's descent into Zurich. Never had a voice sounded so sweet, so honeyed, so full of hope to Gouama. He glanced outside the window. Switzerland was below him. The two towers of Gross-Munster protruded like two great breasts, expressly for his own pleasure. The view broke up the monotony of the Limmat River, which unfurled like a white ribbon through the valley below. The summer had decked out the valley in green dress, shoot through with bright flowers across the fields. The white peaks of the Alps enchanted him even more than the fields in flower. "Switzerland! What a marvelous country!" exclaimed Gouama.

"Blessings upon the Vienna Congress of 1815 which proclaimed the neutrality of this beautiful country and which permits President Gouama today to launch his bid to crush those who usurped his power."

"I feel completely revived, my dear Minister. I am convinced that very soon I will be restored to my rightful place."

"There's no doubt, my dear President. So long as we put every possible means at our disposal."

"No need to crash through an open door. A proverb from my country best sums it up, 'It's not the old woman who must be taught how to satisfy the desires of a man.'"

When Gouama disembarked from the Boeing, he wanted to kiss the earth but was stopped by the Minister. In the taxi that drove him to the Hilton Hotel, Gouama could no longer contain his joy. He sang and played drums against the back of the driver's seat. Before climbing out of the taxi, he gave the driver a hundred dollar tip.

"Garçon," he said to the hotel bellhop. "How many girls are there in your hotel?"

"I beg your pardon, sir?"

"Mr. President, you may call me. I asked you how many girls work in your hotel."

"I'm not sure, Mr. President. What exactly do you mean?"

"I want to know if you can send a girl to my room this evening."

"You mean... You're wanting...."

"I never sleep alone if I can help it."

"Very well, Mr. President, only it is forbidden for us to make arrangements of that nature for our clients."

"But you'll make an exception in my case? I'd like a beautiful young woman, but not a professional. Above all, no professionals. Look around and see what you can find. I'm prepared to pay you handsomely. If anyone asks, I'll say she's my wife."

The bellhop took a step backward, uncertain what to do.

"Get going and find me a girl, I say. I'll give you two thousand U.S. dollars. I'll give you five hundred now for a down payment and the rest when you return. But like I said, no professionals. You got it?"

"Yes, yes, Mr. President."

The bellhop quickly stuffed the bills in his pocket and hurried out of the room. Gouama hopped on the bed without bothering to take off his shoes. "My dear Minister," he said. "What's the name of the imbecile who once said money doesn't buy happiness?"

"I'm not sure, Mr. President, but it was certainly the biggest idiot-savant the world has ever known."

"A Marxist, no doubt." Gouama stretched out further on the bed, lighting a fat cigar. "My dear Minister, this room doesn't have a fraction of the comfort of my guest rooms in Watinbow. When everything is back to normal, I will invite you to take a vacation in my country. You'll agree, no doubt. You'll appreciate the savoir-faire of my citizens. Until that day, go ahead and buy yourself the best bottle of white wine you can find and charge it to me."

When he was alone again, Gouama could not stop singing. He smoked his cigar and stood for a long time, staring at himself in the mirror. He fidgeted with his tie, smiling at his own reflection.

* * *

The next morning at an early hour, Gouama jumped out of bed and began his stretching exercises. His companion from the previous night still slept, completely exhausted. Gouama performed several sets of calisthenics before he climbed into his scalding, morning bath.

The Paradeplatz, the great banking headquarters of Zurich, thronged with people. Gouama and the minister completed their business at the Grand Bank within an hour. They exited the great revolving doors of the bank with smiles on their lips.

"We can return today, Mr. President," said the Minister. "There's much to be done."

"Not today, Mr. Minister. I need a few days of vacation first. It's summertime, and I'd like to spend a few more pleasant hours in the company of Marguerite, the sweet little lady who even now is waiting for me in my room. I contacted the national office of Swiss tourism last night to draw up a list of things to see."

"Mr. President, I really think it'd be wiser if we returned as soon as possible to begin the good fight. Time may be working against us. What's most crucial is the restoration of your power. All the rest can wait."

"You're right. Work before pleasure, as they say. But I still want two more days here. I'm very anxious to regain my power, and now all the conditions are in place to insure it goes smoothly. When I'm back in charge, I'll start everything over at ground zero. To begin, I plan on taking a white wife."

"Mr. President, when the time comes, you can do all of these things. But first we have a fight on our hands. We must get organized."

"You're right, of course. We'll go back tomorrow night."

Before returning to bed, Gouama stopped at a jewelry store where he purchased an enormous diamond ring. Marguerite waited for him. An airline stewardess who was temporarily unemployed, she had worked for the same airline company as her cousin Edward, who had also been laid off and forced to find a new job as a bellhop at the hotel. Marguerite had traveled all over the world and known men of many backgrounds. She had not hesitated for an instant when her cousin had told her of this black president in search of a partner. The timing was right. The beautiful Marguerite had needed no further prompting.

"I will wait for you, Mr. President," she said.

"Without saying a word, Gouama now held up the small box with the ring inside. Marguerite let out a cry of surprise and admiration.

"This is a symbol of our friendship," Gouama said, "which I hope will continue long after today. A friendship stripped to the bare essentials, a completely calculated friendship, you might say. Now, I don't believe in chance. For me, our meeting was no coincidence. It was written that we would come together in this way. It was fate that brought me to Switzerland, that you would lose your job, that your cousin would work for Hilton."

"I thank you with all my heart."

"Thank me with your kisses and leave your heart to play a more important part, a much more important part. I don't know you very well, it's true, but what I want to ask you now is something very serious."

Marguerite set down the box and moved closer to Gouama, her eyes sparkling with excitement, her mouth slightly open. He kissed her passionately.

"Tell me what it is, my president."

"Marguerite, I'd like to ask you a question. Be spontaneous in your response. Don't keep me waiting. I crave spontaneity. It is possible you could live in Africa?"

"I won't answer your question. How can I?"

"I'm returning to my country to regain my power. I had a family, but I'm going to begin my life anew. I offer you all the material happiness you could ever dream of. If it's money you want, I have all you could ever need. You will have all the jewels that you want, all the furs that you want. You can be in charge of your own bank account. You'll be very rich. You will have all the honors due to the wife of a president."

Marguerite thought she must be dreaming. What she had

wanted before coming to the Hilton Hotel was money, enough money to open a small kiosque where she could sell newspapers. To be the wife of a president! She burst into laughter all over again. "You want me to leave with you tomorrow?"

"No, Marguerite. You will join me when I've put my affairs in order. But if you accept, and if you give me your word, I'll set up an account for you, an allowance with a fixed monthly sum."

"You have to let me think about this, at least until your plane leaves tomorrow. All this has turned my head. I'm not an intellectual, you know. I never went to any university. You've said such fantastic things. It seems like I'm dreaming. Let's go talk about this over lunch, my president."

"We will go to the best restaurant in Zurich," Gouama said. "Call and reserve us a table. I'll wake you up from your dream. You'll see that this is no fantasy. It's reality, pure reality. Tell me, Marguerite, how old are you?"

"Thirty-two, Mr. President. Am I too old for you?"

"Not at all. I was merely curious. I'm fifty-seven myself. We must get you a new dress before lunch. You go pick one out while I meet with my friend. I won't dictate the style or color, but I'd like to see you in a dress that shows off your lovely breasts. To whet my appetite for this afternoon. Here's an envelope with some cash. There's plenty for several dresses."

Marguerite hurriedly opened the envelope and stared speechless at its contents. She had never held so much money in her hands before. She left without even thanking Gouama for the gift.

The next day, Gouama returned on Swissair to Zakro, as happy as he'd been the day of his arrival. Marguerite had agreed to marry him, so Gouama opened a bank account for her, promising to supplement it on a monthly basis. The minister had put his foot down when Gouama wanted to make a short trip to Paris. They had to be absolutely discreet, he'd said, and get back to Zakro before Gouama was recognized. Their main objective had been accomplished: Gouama had successfully transferred all his funds to the Central Bank of Zakro, all in an account under the name of Banta Sylla.

The day of his return to Zakro, he asked to meet with President Dagny. The Minister of the Interior repeated to him what he'd said the day of his arrival: "*President Dagny is out of the country, and for national security reasons he cannot enter into contact with anyone other than his immediate family members and me.*"

Perhaps he is gravely ill, Gouama wondered? However, that same night, around two in the morning, he was awoken by the Minister of the Interior. President Dagny had asked to see him at once. Beaming with happiness, Gouama dressed himself in record time. Now, the real fight would begin. President Dagny would no doubt want to offer him his perspective on the best way to restore his throne.

"Where is President Dagny?" he asked the Minister.

"I can only tell you that's not in the capital. Please step into the car. We'll be joining him shortly."

The powerful Mercedez was led by a motorcycle escort which sped through the empty streets of the city. Soon they arrived at a military base.

"You'll continue your journey by plane, Mr. President. Your colleague and brother Dagny awaits you in his palace in the south."

"Wonderful," Gouama said. "I look forward to seeing him, my brave old Dagny, the greatest statesman in all of Africa! That Dagny is a true sage. The people of Zakro are lucky to have such a man at the helm.

"Mr. Minister, I'm not sure how long our discussions will last, but when I return, could you make sure the same girl you sent over tonight is still waiting for me? This one is truly exquisite. Her nice, firm breasts, round ass and thighs! Of course, I'm not telling you all this to encourage you, you old dog!"

The two men burst into laughter.

"Never fear, my President. No one will so much as nibble at your private little feast. She'll be waiting all for you, just as you left her."

"Very good, perfect. All right, let's go see my brother and friend Dagny. If all goes well, by the end of next month, I'll breakfast with the head of that traitor Kodio."

"Have no fear, your Excellency. President Dagny is a capable man. And, you have your money now. Success is certain. In fact, President Dagny is quite impatient to see you. He has been ever since your arrival. Bon voyage, my President. Give my regards to your colleague, our Beloved Father in Zakro. The most intelligent and honest man in all of Africa. A true sage."

Accompanied by two armed guards, Gouama climbed into a small jet airplane, where he was offered a drink and a newspaper. Gouama asked for champagne. "I have to get used to this stuff again," he said, laughing.

Before long, Gouama found himself yawning. He tried to fight off sleep but to no avail. It was late at night, and his head began to nod. Soon he fell fast asleep.

CHAPTER FOURTEEN

Gouama struggled to come to consciousness. How long had he slept? One night? Two nights, perhaps? Where was he? In Switzerland? An airplane? The palace of President Dagny? He sat up and looked around at the room where he now found himself. He felt like he was dreaming. At last, he pulled himself together. He was in a room without furniture. There was only a mattress laid out on the floor. The red brick walls were completely empty and cold. And were was the door? He looked all around but saw no door anywhere. About two meters above his head, there was a naked light bulb protected by a metal cage. There was also a wooden platform with metal hinges.

"Who's there?" he shouted. "Who's there?"

His voice violently echoed off the bare walls. Gouama covered his ears. I'm having a nightmare, he thought. He laid back on the mattress and fell asleep. But when he awoke, the red brick wall was still there, staring him in the face. He put his feet down on the concrete floor. It was hard and cold on his bare feet. There seemed only one way to escape his nightmare: sleep. He lay down again on the mattress, only this time sleep would not come to him. A thousand questions assailed him. If he wasn't dreaming, this could only be reality. President Dagny would surely not receive me in a room like this. He stood up again and stared for a long time at the wall. All at once, he smashed his fist into the wall. A sharp pain shot through his hand. His knuckles and fingers dripped with blood. It was a real wall, all right. This was no dream.

Gouama slowly began to cry. Warm tears flowed down his cheeks. He felt sick at heart. The room began to spin in front of his eyes. He dropped to the ground, nearly unconscious. Above him, the wooden platform swung open and a ladder slid down into the room. Two military guards climbed down the ladder, followed by a man in a white shirt.

"Where am I?" Gouama said. "Who are you? Where is President Dagny?"

"We're here to attend to your wound. You must save your questions for others. We're not authorized to answer them."

The man in the white shirt rapidly examined Gouama's wounded hand. "You have fractured two fingers and dislocated your wrist."

"Where is President Dagny? Where am I? Tell President Dagny I must see him."

"Give me your hand and stop asking idiotic questions."

"But I demand to know. I have the right to know what's going on here. Did our plane crash? Is President Dagny still in power?"

"Turn your hand, slowly."

"I am the President of Watinbow. You must tell me what..."

"Hold out your arm."

"Was our plane rerouted? If you are kidnappers, I have money. I can pay you a ransom if you free me. I must meet with President Dagny. We have urgent matters to discuss."

"Take off your pants. I must give you an injection."

"I am the legitimate President of Watinbow. You owe me an explanation. You must tell me what's going on here."

A vulgar laugh echoed from the platform above them. Gouama began to shiver with nervousness. "Who is that imbecile laughing up there? I am the legitimate President of

Watinbow. I demand respect."

"Drop your pants. We're going to reset your fingers."

"I demand an explanation. Tell me where I am. Tell me who has made me a prisoner here."

"You must keep your arm in a sling we'll provide for you. Above all, you must make no sudden movements."

Gouama grabbed hold of the shirt of the doctor. A violent blow from one of the guards knocked him back to his mattress. The doctor leaned down and wiped the blood from Gouama's mouth. He examined Gouama's mouth and teeth, which bled profusely.

"You'll regret this," Gouama shouted. "My friend Dagny will see that you pay for this."

The guards burst into laughter.

"We will see who has the last laugh," Gouama said.

The two men laughed even harder.

"I've done all I can," the man in the white shirt said. "We can go. I'll set his fingers in plaster this evening."

The man in the white shirt climbed back up the ladder, followed by the two military guards. Gouama tried to follow in his turn, but the guard above him dug his boot into Gouama's good hand. He recoiled in pain, as the laughter echoed above him.

The ladder disappeared, and the wooden platform swung shut. Gouama fell back on the mattress and broke into sobs. His hands throbbed with pain. He could scarcely believe what was happening to him. There could only be one explanation: he had been betrayed by someone in Zakro, which meant that his friend and colleague Dagny had fallen from power.

If this were the case, who was to blame for what had happened? Maybe the coup-makers had taken Dagny hostage? Gouama was prepared to sacrifice his entire fortune to save Dagny and himself if necessary. The only thing he couldn't understand was how Dagny had been deposed, seeing that he was guarded by a foreign army? It seemed impossible. Maybe the coup-makers had failed in their attempt and were seeking to trade Gouama for their own freedom? If this were the case, he would have no choice but to go along with whatever they wanted.

His right hand was now swollen and enflamed. The pain grew even more unbearable.

A few hours later, the man in the white shirt climbed back down the ladder. Gouama had already sobbed for hours, and he was now drowsy. "I've come to set your fingers in plaster," the man said. "But you must not bother me with useless questions."

"It's useless for me to ask questions? To try and find out what's going on? How would you like to be in my situation?"

"Each one of us is in the situation that he deserves, I think. At the moment, I greatly prefer my own."

"I fall asleep in an airplane and wake up in prison, and you tell me my questions are 'useless'? You call this humane treatment?"

"The plaster will help your fingers heal more quickly. But you must keep your arm in the sling at all times."

"Go ahead and do your work, Doctor," said one of the guards. "Each time he asks a question, I'll slug him in the face."

Gouama took a long look at the soldier who had spoken and who now grimaced at him. He decided to keep his mouth shut. When the doctor had finished with him, Gouama fell back on the mattress, which was still wet from his tears. The doctor and his guards climbed back up the ladder. This time, Gouama did not attempt to follow them. A few minutes later, the platform opened up and the ladder descended once again.

"Climb up! Climb! Grab hold of the ladder and climb! Quickly!"

"I can come up?"

"Do as I say. Use your left hand. It's less hurt than the one you smashed against the wall. You should get a medal after that little boxing match."

"Is President Dagny up there?"

"Just climb up, you son of a whore!"

Gouama climbed the ladder, his heart racing. When he reached the top, he found that he was in a luxuriously decorated room. He recognized the paintings hanging on the walls. He had copies of them in his office in Watinbow.

"Come this way," he was told. He was conducted into a furnished room. "You will stay here, until the final day." The military guard left him alone in the room, closing the door behind him. Gouama heard the key turn three times in the lock.

Alone, he glanced around at his new surroundings. The room reminded him of one of his presidential chambers. The radio and television sets, the giant hanging clock, the two large armoires and buffets were all located in the same places as those in the room in Watinbow. The wall clock indicated that it was eight o'clock. He turned on the radio. The broadcaster spoke of the second day of combat along the western border of "our country." Gouama turned on the television but couldn't get any station. At last, he found Radio France International on the radio, but it played only music. He returned to the station he'd found before, where the broadcaster had spoken of "our country."

"Dear Listeners," the broadcaster said. "Pitted against the aggression of imperialist mercenaries, many of the patriots of our country have sent letters of support to our Liberator, our Beloved Guide, to encourage our army to crush these mercenaries and the devil who unleashed them upon us.

"Here's one from the union of transportation in our country: 'Mr. President, confronted with the barbarous aggression of mercenaries in the pay of the former tyrant and assassin of our people, we offer you our complete support. As a token of our support, we place at your disposal 500,000 liters of gasoline and twenty-seven million CFA.

"Here's one from the National Union of Women: 'Mr. President...'" Gouama turned the radio knob back to the station with music. He needed time to sort things out in his mind. Within a few minutes, however, Radio France International began its regular emission, "24 Hours In Africa." Immediately, Gouama turned off the radio. He could get caught up on the news later. Right now, he wanted to stop thinking altogether. He could not seem to shake off this nightmare. However, he could not stop himself from turning the television back on. This time, he found a station that horrified him. It was General Etienne Kodio, the usurper of his power, reading a speech from behind a desk.

Gouama grew furious. Why would a Zakro television station transmit such garbage? He almost turned the television off but then stopped himself: He must let the nightmare play itself out. What if it was all a practical joke of his friend Dagny? To test his nerves? That had to be it. But then he remembered his sufferings in the cell, the soldier who had stepped on his hand. When this bad joke was over, he would give Dagny a piece of his mind. He turned the radio back on and tuned into Radio France International.

"The mercenaries have been derailed. After a second day of bitter combat, pitting the hired soldiers of the deposed president of Watinbow against the Watinbow National Army, the troops of General Kodio have won a decisive military victory. This is what we have learned from our regional correspondent.

"More than a hundred men from the National Army of Watinbow were killed today, while two hundred and sixty mercenaries were killed and another ten captured. After two days of deadly fighting, the national army successfully captured several of the most important military installations of the mercenaries.

"Along the borders of Zakro, the mercenaries had benefited from the cooperation of certain Watinbow businessmen, all supporters of the deposed president Gouama. This morning, the national radio of Watinbow announced the defeat of what it called a 'hoard of mercenaries' in the service of the deposed dictator. In a speech to the nation, General Kodio has just confirmed the defeat of those he called the 'supporters of Satan.'

"Rumors have also circulated that Watinbow's former president has been captured by the national army. These rumors have neither been confirmed nor denied. Certain well-informed sources have reported that the Republic of Zakro has closed its borders with Watinbow, and that elements of Zakro's army have aided in the rescue of the mercenaries.

"A number of letters of support from popular syndicates and leaders in the cities and countryside have been sent to the national radio station to show support for General Kodio and his army. A crowd of volunteers presented itself yesterday at the military garrison in the capital to enlist in the army. Watinbow National Radio announced there will be demonstrations of support in the capital tomorrow. The day has been declared a national holiday.

"The Major Adjunct to the Head of State in Zakro confirmed for me this morning that the mercenaries had failed in their efforts to coordinate their actions. It seems that at least one neighboring country will be implicated in this mercenary operation. We have reports..."

Gouama turned off the radio. Maybe he was losing his mind, he thought? How could such absurd things be happening to him? He searched the room for a hidden speaker system but could find nothing. The broadcast had to be coming from the radio then, not from a hidden speaker.

Dagny will pay for treating me in such a cavalier fashion, he swore. He will pay for this! Gouama stretched out on the bed, but he sat up only moments later. How could he really know if he was crazy or not? Did a crazy man ever really know that he was crazy? And if he wasn't crazy, could what he heard and saw be reality? It wasn't possible. Who had hired the mercenaries, if not he himself? No one could have done it in his absence.

And why was it he had not yet been allowed to meet Dagny? Was Dagny dead? Sick? If he was dead, it would explain the disrespectful treatment he'd received from the guards. For years, he and Dagny had belonged to the same Masonic Lodge, where Gouama had stood as Dagny's personal sponsor. Consequently, it was not possible for Dagny to betray him.

He must pull himself together. A good night's sleep would be helpful, he decided, a first step. He turned off all the lights and crawled under a thick bedspread. But a few minutes later, he climbed out of bed again, turning on all the lights, the radio, the television, and record player. Then he pulled the sheets and covers off the bed, knocking lamps and other items onto the floor. He tried to open the two large armoires but they were locked. He picked at the lock with a sharp-edged, metal ashtray.

He looked for something more useful to pick the lock when General Kodio appeared once again on the television screen. At that moment, the ashtray snapped in the lock, breaking with a loud crack. The door to his room opened and the two military guards stood looking at him. "Have you gone crazy?" One of the men said. "Jean, call the general and give him an update."

"Who are you? Where is President Dagny? What sort of bad joke is this?"

"I don't have to answer to you," the soldier said, holding his fist in Gouama's face. He walked over and yanked the television plug out of the wall.

Gouama addressed him again, this time in a more humble tone. "Tell me, please. Am I crazy? Am I dead? What country am I in? Tell me, please. Is this a dream? I am the President of Watinbow. I will pay you well for your efforts."

The soldier looked at him for a long moment. "You have money hidden here?"

"Not here, but in the Central Bank. I..."

"You haven't hidden money in your bedroom?"

"Well, yes, but in my bedroom in Watinbow, not here. If you..."

"Try to describe to me where you hid your money."

"It's useless. If I were in Watinbow, I could tell you. But I have money here in Zakro. If you answer my questions, I'll pay you well. Tell me what's going on."

"Not until you tell me where you hid your money in Watinbow. I want to know the exact place in the Presidential Palace."

"Have you ever been to Watinbow? Do you even know what the Presidential Palace looks like?"

"None of that matters. Tell me where you've hidden the money, and I'll tell you what it is you want to know."

"You swear it?"

"I'll swear by any name you want."

"Swear on your honor and by God."

"I swear on my honor and by God as my witness to tell President Gouama all that he wants to know if he'll tell me where he hid his money in the Presidential Palace."

"Very well. Bring me a pen and paper and I'll draw you a map of the Presidential Palace."

Once seated at the desk, Gouama sketched out a map for the soldier. "Here is the airport of the Capital of Watinbow."

"I know the capital well enough."

"Okay. In my office at the Presidential Palace, there is a large chandelier. In the crook of the chandelier's chains, there is a small crank-handle. But you'll need a ladder to reach it."

"Go on."

"You must turn the crank twelve times. Twelve full rotations. This will open a small strong box in the wall of the shower. You will find there money and gold. The day we arrive in Watinbow, I will..."

The soldier abruptly left the room. Gouama heard the key turn three times in the lock. He was now completely befuddled. Large tears welled in his eyes. What kind of world was this? A world of madmen, no doubt. At least he was convinced now that he was not crazy himself. He picked up a magazine that the soldier had left behind after departing so quickly and read a page at random in a loud voice. He wasn't crazy. Crazy people don't know how to read, he told himself. But to be on the safe side, he read the entire page aloud. Then he remembered a crazy man he once knew who could read, a professor who had gone mad.

Gouama collapsed on the bed again and burst into tears. In the midst of his blubbering, the door opened. It was the soldier who had sworn to answer all his questions, now beaming with joy. "I've brought you something to eat," he said. "I even added a liter of whiskey, a personal gift from me to you. But I poured it all in a plastic bottle, to make sure you wouldn't try and kill yourself."

"You promised to tell me what's happening."

"And so I will. But now's not the time. First you must calm down. Everything will be fine. I'll tell you everything you want to know tomorrow."

Gouama remained in a state of bewilderment. He got up anyway and began drinking the whiskey. He could feel the alcohol coursing through his veins, warming his heart and internal organs. He was not hungry. The pain from his wounds made his hands throb, but the alcohol brought on forgetfulness. He drank more than half a litre before falling asleep.

When he awoke, he quickly drank the remaining whiskey. He stumbled about the room for awhile before picking up the magazine again and trying to read. A group of five armed soldiers entered the room. When they told him they were there to interrogate him, Gouama did his best to steel himself. "Mr. Gouama, quickly change into this military uniform," he was commanded.

Gouama raised his eyes to look up at the soldier who had tossed him the uniform. "But I'm not a soldier," he said. "I'm the President of the Republic."

"No more pointless discussion. Get dressed now. If you refuse, we will dress you ourselves."

Gouama set down his magazine. He had not even bothered to undress since boarding the plane. His broken fingers had hurt him too badly. One of the soldiers helped him change into the uniform. He looked at himself in the mirror and broke into laugher. For the first time since his flight to see Dagny, he felt the desire to laugh.

"I lack only a pistol to complete my disguise," he said. "Now I know that I've gone crazy. But at least I know it, which is more than you men can say. Don't you see, we are all bit players in a grotesque comedy. The difference is that I know it and you don't."

"Here is your pistol and holster. The gun has of course been emptied of its bullets."

The man in the white shirt entered the room. He gave Gouama an injection in one arm. Almost at once, the room began to spin in front of Gouama's eyes. The soldiers carried him outside and put him in a military jeep. His feet were wedged into a pair of leather military boots and sat against the floor of the jeep. A seatbelt held him in place in the backseat of the vehicle. He now sat upright, surrounded by other soldiers.

It seemed to Gouama that the jeep was moving. Everything blurred around him. His ears buzzed. It seemed to him that an immense crowd of people was lined up along both sides of the road. Was the crowd shouting? Possibly. The only thing he could be certain of was that the crowd parted like waves of breaking water. The jeep kept moving forward. For how long? One hour, maybe three. Time seemed to stand still. Maybe he was dead? It hardly seemed to matter anymore.

When he awoke, he was back in his room, his head heavy like a block of wood. He reached for the plastic bottle of whiskey, but it was empty. The clock read nine o'clock. He got up and knocked on the door. A soldier opened it.

"What do you want?"

"Whiskey, please," he said.

A few minutes later, the soldier returned with a bowl of rice and another plastic bottle filled with whiskey.

"Please," Gouama said. "Tell me what's happening to me."

"Turn on your television and listen to the radio. But don't tear up anything else." The soldier left.

Gouama greedily drank the whiskey and turned on the television. A group of soldiers in a jeep drove through an hysterical crowd of shouting people. The jeep drove very slowly. What a strange resemblance! The soldier in the middle looked just like him. He even wore a cast on one of his hands, which stuck out from a sling. Gouama drank more whiskey. The camera angle switched to a close up. There could be no doubt. The soldier in the middle was him. He realized that even now he wore a military uniform.

A television commentator intervened: "Dear viewers, you have just seen the entry into the capital of the tyrant and traitor Gouama, the assassin and head of the mercenary army. We will see now the work of this devil who, after raping, pillaging, and torturing our people, paid his army of mercenaries with money stolen from us." The television screen now displayed images of mutilated and burnt bodies, many of them charred beyond recognition. "This is the work of the demonic tyrant Gouama.

"We will now hear from the President of our Great Nation."

General Kodio appeared on the screen in full military regalia. Dozens of shiny medals covered his breast. Gouama did his best to remain calm, drowning two more swigs of whiskey and laying back on the bed.

"My dear compatriots," Kodio said. "It is with a bitter heart that we have turned back the ignoble attack of the mercenaries against our people. Our armed forces have suffered the loss of one hundred and twenty men and many more have been wounded. We have succeeded in killing more than two hundred and seventy mercenaries and are still routing out others.

"The sacrifice of our valiant soldiers, fallen on the field of honor, now demands three things of us: unity, organization, and hard work.

"Our losses today should bring us together more than ever before. Watinbow will henceforth be regarded around the world as a strong and united country. History will record the great victory and determination of our people today. All the world will know we are a free and prosperous people.

"But we must also regard this victory as a mandate to organize. Organization is the greatest richness possessed by mankind. Despite our differences, we must set aside our prejudices and embrace one another as a common people, united in the desire to better ourselves and our country.

"Each of us must ask ourselves a simple question: What would have happened had this hoard of foreign murderers invaded our country? We need only reflect upon the injuries suffered by so many of us in the last two days to find an answer.

"We must also pause for a moment to consider the role in these atrocities played by certain of our countrymen. To safeguard their personal interests, certain businessmen, civil servants, and even military men collaborated with these assassins of our people. Rest assured they will be punished for their crimes. Justice will be served. Without hatred, without passion, but with rigor and finality.

"You have all seen today the author of these crimes. He has shamed all of us, for the outside world can now say, 'Do you see how the people of Watinbow mercilessly slaughter one another to stay in power?' Most of us would have laid down our lives to spare the families who are grieving today what they are now going through. But we could not evade our responsibility to bring this tyrant to heel, this diabolical assassin who sought to conquer us with his foreign army.

"Two conclusions can be drawn from these events: First, it is clear we have no choice but to further postpone our return to normal, constitutional life in Watinbow. And, second, we must completely reorganize the military once again.

"Dear compatriots, we urge you to be vigilant at all costs. We have succeeded in capturing Gouama, the commander of the mercenaries. But as you know, he was well supported by those who still would like to pillage and subjugate our people. He will be judged by a military court as well as an ordinary tribunal.

"Long live our valiant army! Long live our glorious people! Long live Watinbow!"

CHAPTER FIFTEEN

Gouama slept. He had succeeded in shutting down his mental processes, in convincing himself that he really was crazy. The world that he occupied could not possibly be real. He merely waited patiently for things to return to normal. The nightmare would have to end sooner or later. When he awoke, he found that his room teemed with men in military dress.

"Mr. Gouama, the military tribunal awaits its first interview with you."

"Military tribunal?" Gouama rapidly washed his face, even brushing his teeth with one finger.

"There is no time to lose," a soldier said. "The court has no time to waste."

The court? Gouama's heart began to palpitate. He felt like he was having a heart attack. Suddenly, he slumped to the floor. The president of the court was none other than President Kodio, the President of the Republic of Watinbow.

When Gouama opened his eyes, the man in the white shirt stood over him. The members of the court were still in their places.

"You'll find that fainting will get you no where, Mr. Gouama. Take your seat. The court has a number of questions for you."

Gouama was helped to his feet and ushered to a chair that was prepared for him. Between his chair and those of the court sat a soldier stationed behind a machine gun, aimed directly at him.

"Leave him be," the judge said. "It's obvious he poses no threat to anyone in his present condition."

Gouama did not even pay attention to the machine gun, which was pointed at his breast. He was himself anxious to figure out what was happening to him, what was the meaning of these extraordinary events. He sat like a statue, waiting to see what would happen.

"My name is General Kodio, President of the Republic of Watinbow, Minister of the Defense, President of the Military Court which will judge you. The other members of this court are all members of the Advisory Committee of the Military Committee that is presently directing this country. Before speaking of your crimes against the people, we will first discuss the subject of your illegal wealth. We want to know everything about the money and other assets you have amassed since coming to power."

"I will not tell you anything until you tell me how it is that I came here."

"You came here in an airplane. How could you not know this? An airplane with wings that flies in the air. You boarded a Foker plane in Zakro at three in the morning."

"And how did I end up here, since my destination was a city in Zakro, where I was supposed to meet President Dagny?"

"You were misled about the destination. It's as simple as that."

Gouama sighed. So that was it. The pilot had taken him in the wrong direction. But maybe not all was lost, he said to himself. Kodio and the others wanted to know about his money. He could still ransom his life and his freedom.

"My money is in Switzerland and in Zakro. But to get it, I have to be physically present. President Dagny is guarding my checking account for me."

The members of the court snickered with laughter. Gouama

felt his heart sink. The cynical laughter of the court was not a good sign. He took a deep breath before speaking again: "My money is in a safe place, if that satisfies you."

The court's laughter faded. Kodio suddenly scowled. "Enough bullshit. We've wasted enough time as it is. Gouama, your Swiss bank account was number 22 42 30, in the Grand Bank of Zurich. You transferred the funds from this account to the Central Bank of Zakro. Your bank account number in Zakro is 78-725, under the name of Banta Sylla. The small account you opened for Marguerite Sauvy in Switzerland doesn't interest us. Here is the checkbook from your account in the Central Bank of Zakro."

Gouama tried to pick up the checkbook that Kodio tossed at him. The man in the white shirt bent over to get it for him.

"Should we continue, Gouama? Or are you going to waste more of the court's time?" Kodio's tone was grave and menacing.

"What we want to know are the numbers of your bank accounts in France, the United States, and Watinoma. We already have a list of your property in Europe. Don't waste our time speaking of the money you hid in your bath room. We got that already."

Gouama remained silent, determined not to give up.

"Maybe you're waiting for help still? Perhaps from your old friend Dagny? Let me clarify the situation for you. I signed an accord with your friend and colleague Dagny. It's thanks to him that we have you with us today. You know that he's president of the administrative council of the powerful diamond society, which has outposts all over the continent. We have agreed to cede the very rich diamond field discovered ten years ago in the north of Watinbow. Yes, it's been ten years since this diamond field was discovered, only you were never informed of its existence.

"I ceded this mine to my colleague Dagny of Zakro in exchange for you, plus 15% of the profits and an agreement for military assistance. So from Dagny, you can expect nothing. You can see very well that he gave us your checking account.

"All those who might have helped you have either been killed or paid off. In the coming days, those we have under arrest will make full confessions. The well-advertised mercenary aggression that we stage with certain elements of Zakro's army was a way of routing out those who remained loyal to you. We have also arrested the businessmen and all your relatives who were implicated in the mercenary action that you hoped to organize."

The court began to laugh all over again.

"You cannot count on the support of the Ambassador or your advisor Marcel, since it was they who initiated the coup to begin with. In the beginning, we hesitated, but they convinced us when Marcel gave us proof that you wanted to sign an accord with several Marxist countries. To bring Marxism here to Watinbow!

"You cannot even hope that the Watinbow people are indifferent to your fate. If we were to set you free today, the people would hunt you down and burn you alive. I'm not even sure your own family would take you in. Your wife, in any case, has become infatuated with a young soldier, a guard at your house. We've even got proof for you, so you won't have to take our word for it. Corporal, bring in the video player and put in that tape."

Gouama saw his wife in a passionate embrace with a young soldier in their bedroom at the palace. When she began to take off her clothes, he thought he was going to faint once again. But he got a grip on himself when he heard his wife call him him an 'egotist' and 'assassin' in the midst of their love-making.

"Turn it off!" Kodio barked. "You see, Gouama? She had your children all come to me and beg forgiveness, which I readily accepted. I explained to them that they were not to blame for their father's sins. They fully understand the crimes you have committed. They know what kind of man you are. They have seen the dried-out human tongues and human hearts in your room. They've also seen your collection of human bones. And so you see, Gouama, you are completely alone. You don't have a friend in the world.

"No, wait, I forgot your faithful advisor Tiga. He sent us two hundred million CFA as a contribution to help in the building of hospitals and health-units in Watinbow.

"To sum up, if you give us a full accounting of all your holdings, you just might leave here without being tortured."

"There's nothing more to tell," Gouama shrugged, "which is just as well. So do with me what you will. I deserve everything that happens to me. I can see now that I lacked a clear vision of the world and of my society. As the Romans put it, 'So much for the vanquished!' The defeated always get what's coming to them."

"Enough useless philosophizing. The only thing that interests is your money."

"If I had known better, I might have used that money to alleviate the sufferings of my people, in building schools and health units. I don't say this now to gain mercy from you or anyone else. None of that interests me."

"You have nothing to fear, Gouama. You'll get no mercy from any of us. Sooner or later, you'll tell us what we want to hear. We also want to know who helped you escape."

"I wasn't home during the coup. I had a meeting with one of my sorcerers outside the city. When I heard the gunfire, I fled. The sorcerer and I traveled across the bush together, after we drove our car into a river. My companion is now in Watinoma."

"Enough chit-chat! Where is the rest of your money?"

"I don't have any more money. Our country is not as rich as you seem to think. The accounts you've already gotten hold of are the most I was able to scrape together out of foreign aid money and international loans. But I could tell you splendid tales of great wealth, if it'd make you feel better..."

"That's precisely what you will do, Mr. Gouama. Go ahead, we're all waiting."

"Unfortunately, the wealth that I have to share cannot be measured in strict cash terms. What I can give you is a wealth of advice. First, I would..."

A fist smashed into Gouama's nose, sending him sprawling to the floor. He lay flat for a moment but struggled back to his feet. There was not a single tear in his eyes. He calmly surveyed the members of the tribunal, as if he hid some momentous secret. His composure intrigued the court.

"Well done, Mr. Gouama!" Kodio said. "You took that blow without wincing. I'm impressed."

"I propose now to offer you the rarest of treasures," Gouama said softly. "A treasure to end all treasures."

The soldier who had struck him moved closer, his hands clenching into fists.

"Let him say what he has to say," Kodio said. "It won't help him any, and it may bring us pleasure. After all, the cat enjoys playing with its prey before devouring it, does it not?"

Gouama smiled. "I tell you now that real wealth, the only true riches a man should strive to attain, especially a man who seeks to be a spokesman for his people, is to gain a place within the history of his people, to not be excluded from that history. The age of a man should not be counted in years but in the services he has performed for his people. And so I say to you now, it's not too late for each one of you to come clean, to start anew. But for those of you without ears to hear, may you get the miserable life that you deserve!"

"So you've become a philosopher, now that you've lost your power. You presume to lecture to the rest of us."

"I've been a philosopher for a long time, President Kodio. This is why I never betrayed my friends. I always remembered those who helped me. And I've never committed perjury."

President Kodio suddenly jumped up. His chair came crashing down on Gouama's head, who was unable to duck in time. "Get up, you son of a bitch!" Kodio shouted.

Gouama struggled to climb to his feet, his body numb with pain. A thin trickle of blood ran down his forehead. "I give you back the kick you once gave me when you played at being president." Kodio violently kicked Gouama in the stomach with his heavy military boots. The kick sent Gouama sprawling across the floor. The General reached down and pulled Gouama up by his shirt collar. "Get up you filthy bastard! You son of a whore! Take this book!"

Gouama wiped away the blood that spurted from his nose and took hold of the book that Kodio held out to him.

"Open it to the cornered page and read the sentence underlined in red. Read it quickly, you son of a bitch!"

Gouama wiped away more blood and read, "*When princes think of their personal pleasures more than their armies, they have as good as lost their kingdoms.*"

"Do exactly what I tell you to do. Read the second marked page."

"*There can be no real law and order where there is no military power.*"

"Continue!"

"*A prince should therefore have no other goal, no other thought, nor take up any other art, besides the art of war, as well as the institutions and science of warfare; for this is the only art that is fitting for a ruler.*" Gouama closed the book and smiled at Kodio. He continued. "In writing 'The Prince,' Machiavelli wanted to make one main point about the exercise of power, a point that was appropriate for his era. In the very same book, he wrote, '*All wordly things must come to an end sooner or later, but the machinations of power require that the reason for their coming and going are soon forgotten.*'"

"Silence!" A fist in the face knocked Gouama onto the floor once again.

"Leave him be, General," said one of the officers. "He'll get what's coming to him soon enough."

"Let me say a few more words to him before he dies. A man who is staring at death can become a veritable oracle. Gouama, have you had any dreams since we brought you here? Any visions?"

The occasion was ripe: Gouama seized the opportunity without hesitating. "I've had many dreams. Last night, I dreamed I was in the Central Marketplace in the city. All the women there were nude, like Eve in the Garden of Eden."

"Or like your wife underneath her guard!"

"They were seated on a pile of clothes and selling food on great big platters with placards that read 'Misery With Corruption Sauce,' 'Fried Misery With Sweat,' 'Misery Stew à la Prostitution,' 'Ground Misery With Dictator Sauce'..."

"Enough with your bullshit miseries. Tell us the point of all this."

"After the marketplace, I continued walking towards the butchershop. The butchershop was at the university. Many living animals were for sale there. The sign outside said 'Butchershop' but it seemed more like a slaughterhouse. The customers bought living animals that they killed and cut into pieces. Then they would take the animals' hides and leave the meat behind."

"None of this interests us. How does this concern Watinbow?"

"I saw angry crowds lynching false prophets. I saw a referendum passed, voicing the true will of the people. I helped count the votes myself..."

"He's talking about today's court."

"No, he said it was 'the people' who had voted."

"That's enough, Captain," Kodio said. "Don't you see he's making fools of us. Gouama, we don't need to learn moral lessons from you of all people, not about the nation's future, or about Africa's future. Corporal, go to my office and bring

164

me back a copy on my desk of *Afrique Nouvelle*, Number 598, January 23, 1959. We're going to demonstrate to Gouama today that he is indeed a perjurer."

The corporal came back a few moments later, holding a journal. Kodio opened the journal and read, *"I swear on my honor, for the respect and dignity of Africa, to defend everywhere the Federation of Mali, I swear it. And for the Federation of Mali, for political unity, for African unity, I am prepared to make the ultimate sacrifice if necessary, without hesitation, I swear it.'*

"Gouama, take a good look at this photo. Here you are among those gathered on January 14, 1959 in Bamako. Look closely, there you are. Tell us now, Gouama, what happened to the so-called Federation of Mali? What happened to African Political Unity? It seems to me you aren't in much of a position to accuse anyone here of perjury."

Gouama smiled and said calmly. "The diabolical maneuverings of international imperialism to balkanize Africa are remarkable and subtle. You haven't been in power very long, Kodio. You can't expect to understand how it all works in one day. To analyze and understand the true history of Africa, you need much more experience, a certain intellectual background. That may be too much to ask of you. It takes far more than a beret and a pistol to turn a fool into a wise man."

Kodio set down his gun. Gouama soon blacked out from the flurry of blows and kicks that followed. When he awoke, he found himself laid out upon a table. He was tied down with nylon straps and completely naked. Two giants with fierce scowls stared down at him.

"I have no money hidden anywhere," he said. "I've already told them everything. You're going to torture me for nothing."

"Not for nothing, Gouama. It will give us a great deal of pleasure. A man must amuse himself from time to time." The man who spoke seized hold of Gouama's penis and wrapped an electric wire around it, which was then coiled around his waist. One end of the wire was inserted into his anus while the other was connected to breaker switch.

"Let's see if it's working," one of them said.

Gouama screamed with all his might. He vomited. Diarrhea gushed from underneath him. The filthy wire that was inserted in his anus was now wedged into his urethra.

"Don't do it!" Gouama screamed. "Stop! I'll tell you everything!"

"We can't stop now. We have to give you at least two jolts. I always give at least two jolts to get things going, even with women."

With the second jolt, Gouama blacked out. When he returned to consciousness, he found that Kodio and his companions now surrounded him, a notebook in hand.

"All right, Gouama. Are you ready to talk?"

"I'm ready. I'm seriously ready," he murmured. "I have money in the United States, at the Boston Bank. Only I keep my checkbook stored in a Swiss bank. I have to be there myself to get it."

"Give us the numbers of the accounts."

"My presence is required to open the safety deposit box in Switzerland."

"How much money is in your account?"

"More than a million U.S. dollars."

"Now that's what I like to hear. A fortune. We'll have to verify that, of course." Kodio reached for a wall phone and rapidly dialed a number. "Hello, Mr. Marcel? This is President Kodio. The imbecile's now telling us he has an account at the Boston Bank in the United States, but his checkbook for this account is stored in a safety deposit box at a Swiss bank."

"I see, so he's lying again. I assure you he'll soon tell us the truth. It seems we'll have to be more persuasive."

"I'm telling the truth," Gouama moaned. "I swear to God. Marcel wasn't aware of this account. I kept him completely in the dark. You'd do well to follow my example with him. Kodio.

Listen to me. I know I'm going to die, but I don't want to suffer anymore. Please, if you wish, your Excellency, I'll write out a will and leave you everything I own. Just give me a few minutes to recover from this, so I don't forget anything."

The room became silent. The members of the court quietly conferred, away from the table.

"Bring him to his room and give him whatever he asks for. But Gouama," Kodio said. "Don't think we'll wait forever."

Gouama was carried to his room and laid out on his bed. The tears would no longer come to his eyes. He had seen too many horrors. Too much human ingratitude. He would have liked to tell the entire world about his sufferings, about the ingratitude and spitefulness of man.

Betrayal: this is all that man is really capable of.

The memory of Mamadou and the fishermen drifted back to him. He remembered the advice of Mamadou, who had tried to warn him. It was too late now.

An idea suddenly came to him. He asked to speak privately with Kodio.

"What do you want with me, Gouama? You want to tell me more lies?"

Gouama merely smiled. It was time to play his final card. "Your Excellency," he said, "before I die, there are certain things I must tell you..."

"Tell me, but if you're looking for absolution, you're wasting your time."

"No, your Honor. I don't merit forgiveness from one such as you. As you said it so well, I'd only be wasting my time. But before I die, I wish to obtain from you two favors. First, I want you to marry my daughter Chantal. Second, I ask that you, and you alone, inherit all my worldly goods. That is all that I have to say to you. Do not refuse a condemned man his dying wish. You probably think I'm trying to save myself, to get you to spare me. You are mistaken, your Excellency. I have lived my life. Now, I only want my daughter to live. If you don't want an official marriage, take her as your mistress. With the things you'll inherit from me, you'll be very happy. I will sign a fake will in front of the military committee, but it is to you alone that I will leave all my worldly goods."

President Kodio stood silent for a moment, deep in thought. Gouama took advantage of his silence. "My president," he said, "I want you to carefully consider before giving me an answer."

"It's not necessary. I accept, but..."

"No, there's nothing to add, your Excellency," said Gouama. "I am a happy man. I offer you all my gratitude. May God bless my son-to-be and give him long life, I mean many years in power. Now bring me one of my seals to make this official."

President Kodio exited the room, as Gouama sat at the desk to draw up a will. His rear-end was so sore he needed two pillows to sit on. In the will, he left his entire fortune to his oldest daughter Chantal. He then wrote out a second will leaving all his worldly goods to the Military Committee, represented by Lieutenant Samuel Nongowe, an influential member of the committee. Afterwards, he drank a strong shot of whiskey and let out a long whistle under his breath. He was satisfied.

Would President Kodio allow such a generous father-in-law to be executed? He might very well pardon the man whose blood would be intermingled with those of his own children. A soldier entered.

"You want something to eat, Mr. Gouama?"

"I'll let the cook surprise me. Only, I'd like my meal to be accompanied by a good wine. While I'm waiting, I'd like a strong whiskey over ice."

"Right away, Mr. Gouama," the soldier said, smiling.

Gouama also smiled. Maybe he had succeeded in saving his skin, after all? All hope was not lost. The proof? They brought him everything he needed. After several shots of whiskey, he became even more enthusiastic. He began to dream about his freedom. Kodio will certainly find one reason or another to defend him before the committee. He need only delay the date of the trial. The people have such a short memory, they would no doubt forget his worst crimes in time.

The more that Gouama drank, the more evident it seemed to him that he had saved his life by making this proposition to Kodio. He congratulated himself for coming up with such a brilliant idea. To celebrate his success, he emptied the entire bottle of whiskey. He fell asleep with a light heart.

An hour later, he was awoken by a sharp pain on his left cheek.

"Finally he awakes! We thought you were already dead, Mr. Gouama. That's why we burned you with the cigarette. Nothing else seemed to work. "It was Kodio, standing over him and looking down. "I came to say adieu. The Military Committee has decided that you are to be shot in one hour."

Gouama immediately sat up in bed. The alcohol and sleepiness had completely dissipated.

"My president and lord, Kodio! My god Kodio! Save me! I'll do anything you say." Gouama fell down on his knees and sobbed as he licked Kodio's boots.

"Get up, Gouama. We didn't take all these risks capturing you, so you could walk out of here alive. Everything has its risks in this third world of ours, as you know. The people are capable of burning at the stake today the very same person they loved yesterday. They build up their tyrants and heroes, only so they can tear them down later. Our people are like widows, my friend. Ninety-nine percent of the time they miss their old husbands, even if the new one is far nicer. So, you see, why should I take any chances by keeping you alive?

"Those who are clamoring for your head today will be the first ones to forgive you tomorrow, to find excuses for your crimes. 'He was a good president, after all,' they'll say. 'It was his advisors who led him astray.' No telling what they'd say to turn a devil like you into an angel. We can't always keep such idiots from finding hidden virtues in you. It'll happen anyway. We just prefer that it happens posthumously.

"I've now promised to marry your daughter. Well, I must say it's a shame I'm obliged to execute you, my future father-in-law. You know better than I do that it's nothing personal. It's just politics. It's an old African law that one must kill all those who get in the way. It seems screwy, but that's politics for you!

"So anyway, Gouama, I wish you much courage in this final ordeal. Is there anything else you have to say?"

Gouama cried with all his remaining strength. "Have pity on me," he sobbed. "For God's sake, I don't want to die. Have pity on me. I want to live." He clutched hold of Kodio's knees and wept, until Kodio was forced to push him away.

"We'll be back in thirty minutes," Kodio said, winking at a soldier on his way out.

CHAPTER SIXTEEN

Alone, Gouama began to pace the room. The wall clock read 4:27. There had to be some way to escape. He tapped on the walls but heard no echo. There was nothing he could do. He was to be shot like a common criminal, after having known glory, honors, and happiness. No, it simply could not be possible. He screamed at the top of his lungs.

What good had it done him to be president for all these years? None at all. A little piece of metal would put an end to everything.

Life, true life, happens in a flash, a fleeting moment on a dark night. One hour of suffering can wipe out a century of happiness.

Was he really going to die? It wasn't possible! He pushed back one of the armoire's looking for a secret passageway. It was hard, his fate. If he'd only known, he would have built a secret passageway under the presidential palace. A simple act like that would have saved his life. But now it was over, finished!

If only he could make himself invisible! He remembered rejecting a magical boubou that Tiga has said would make him invisible. He remembered Tiga had also once offered him a magical potion that was supposed to render him impervious to bullets. He had drank the potion but had no confidence in it now. It was better than nothing, of course, but what he really needed was to avoid the firing squad altogether. He searched the room for a hiding place.

Footsteps sounded outside the door. Quickly, Gouama scrambled under the bed. He listened as the door opened and the footsteps grew louder. From under the bed, he could see the black boots of the soldiers.

"It's time, Mr. Gouama. Where are you?"

Gouama remained completely still.

"Okay, Gouama, so we're going to play hide-and-seek, are we? Well,   let's get to it, boys. Time is of the essence. Soon it'll be daylight and very hot. It's better to travel in the morning when it's still cool, especially when you have a long drive ahead of you."

From under the bed, a sob escaped from Gouama's throat. He pleaded once again for mercy, even for a life-sentence in prison. His pleas were in vain. Two of the soldiers bent down and grabbed hold of one of his legs and arms, dragging him out from under the bed. Gouama howled like a wounded animal.

When he saw the truck filled with armed soldiers, he blacked out once again. This time the man in the white shirt was not there to help him.

Gouama did not return to consciousness until they had already arrived at the firing range. The sun had begun to rise, coloring the horizon purple and orange. The birds chirped happily to welcome the new day, but for Gouama it seemed a particularly cruel requiem. His ears buzzed and his sight blurred.

But he could see well enough to notice a man walking towards him. It was a man he knew very well. How many millions of francs had he given this man? This man with his long, black robe who walked with such slow, certain steps? Gouama had just enough energy remaining to explode in one final crisis of anger.

"Get away from me, Satan! Leave me to die in peace, you devil! I will see you in hell, you and all those like you. I'll be waiting for you. I curse you! A thousand curses upon you! Your turn will come, you devil! You will pay, just as I have!

"Paul, you are no priest. You are a devil. You, your bishop, your cardinal, and all the others like you. You who urged me to fight..."

A soldier rapidly gagged Gouama's mouth. A hood was placed over his head. Gouama struggled with all his might to spit out the gag. He longed to fill the world with his cries of hatred and resentment. He nearly succeeded, before the fall of a brutal silence.